THE PROMISCUOUS TRAVELER

Sebastian V. became a world traveler as a young teen, growing up with his family in numerous countries in Asia and the Pacific. Since then, he has journeyed to nearly 80 countries and all seven continents.

Always the outsider, he has learned how to instinctively grasp foreign worlds and read the cultural languages of men and their primal desires.

The Promiscuous Traveler

Sebastian V.

BRUNO GMÜNDER

1st edition
© 2012 Bruno Gmünder Verlag GmbH
Kleiststraße 23-26, D-10787 Berlin
info@brunogmuender.com
© Sebastian V.
Cover art: Steffen Kawelke
Cover photo: © Fred Goudon (from *Virility*), www.fredgoudon.com
Printed in South Korea

ISBN 978-3-86787-443-4

More about our books and authors:
www.brunogmuender.com

Contents

Prologue

ravel and sex. Peanut butter and jelly. Sonny and Cher. Syphilis and penicillin. It's a classic combo.

Cavemen wandered in search of food, to expand their primal footprint. The conquistadors were starving for silver and gold. Men walked on the moon just to prove they could. What possible purpose could traveling serve the human being in his modern form, besides his ego? You can hop on a jet, and in a few hours you'll be magically transported from one world into another, via sitting in some sort of celestial microwave oven housed in a long metal cylinder. You disembark into a different reality, with all the sensual potentials—the smells, the visuals, the tastes, the living flesh of other humans waiting to be touched. You feel heightened. You feel, you smell, you taste, you arouse, you cum. You had an experience. You're satisfied. Promises have been met, the brochure didn't lie.

You have a story to retell—if you were able to capture it at all as it slipped through your fingers.

You move on, you move back to where you came from. You hope the place is still there when you get back, as you left it, wherever it is. Your movement was back and forth, to the place you visited and back. It was movement without progress? That thing you tasted, that person you smelled. The sun on your face. Was it all real? Did you take it back with you somewhere under your skin? Did it mix in with your DNA? Did it leave a lasting mark, or will it all fade away like your careful tan lines?

I hate going back to the same place twice. I'm spoiled. I'm a travel writer. I've been doing this since my twenties, and I've been traveling to foreign countries since I was twelve years old. It's so much a part of my reality that I don't know my life otherwise. My fate is to wander, to wander. Everyone thinks it's so glamorous. It's what they really want to do. What they dreamed about doing. Can I tell them what it's like, how to break into it? Any tips? Please, anything? They want it, the *glamorous* life. Like all things with the word "glamor" dangling from it, it's not nearly as *glamorous* as it looks, or as others want it to be. It's expensive, it's tiring, it's frustrating, it's teasing, it's fleeting. It's life—it's gone. It merely hints at how colossally huge and truly unfathomable the world is, how you will never be able to see it all or get to the end of it, ever. It's depressing at times. It's disconcerting. It's like a dream. And yes, it's a drug.

These pages are a diary, a confessional, a record of what happened, to somehow make it all real and permanent—these unreal and transient moments. The tales are fantastical and masturbatory, but the facts are as solid and honest and unforgiving as the earth.

I've got to see over seventy countries, and have sexual encounters in most of them. Even Greenland, even Antarctica—the ends of the planet. They're in this book, like a record of attempting sex in space, trying to live out the most primordial needs in the most inhuman of settings. I've had sex on trains, on boats, in speeding cars—in a horse carriage for God's sake. (But oddly, now that I think of it, never on a plane. Does an unfinished under-the-blanket hand job by a swarthy Brazilian flight attendant on a Varig flight back from Rio count?)

Yes, I know, it all makes me a slut, I get it. I'm one small step up from a male stewardess, a *trolly dolly*. I accept it. I am a promiscu-ous traveler. And the title is that on two accounts. The first reason is a little more oblique: I never like to go back to the same place twice. The second is more traditional: I've tasted so many different types of men. Young, old, big, small, brown, black, white, straight, gay, or simply just men. I appreciate all the tastes of all the cui-sines of the world. I want to feel their energy towards me, to feel their energy radiate through their skin to mine, like metal warm-ing metal. I want to smell their hair, taste the flavor and texture of their ejaculate. I want to be a special specimen for them, some American variety of human they've always fantasized about but never had. From the movies, from TV, from the web sites, from wherever modern dreams derive. I want to be as exotic as they are to me. I want to serve myself up as a dish for them to devour. And they are devoured in return.

I have a huge appetite for the world. I want to know what every-one is like, what is around the next bend. I don't want to leave the Earth without having had a good taste of it.

And I sadly recognize I will never get to the end of my quest.

Orbis non sufficit, as Alexander the Great's tombstone and James Bond's coat of arms tell us so succinctly. *The world is not enough.*

And like those two pinnacles of portable promiscuity, I am al-ways the trick and never the husband. I also know I will never experience what I am supposed to. I understand this is my fate.

Cavemen, after all, knew their territory, knew the changing of the seasons, knew their plants, knew their place within the cos-mos. It's in our human DNA to come from somewhere, to be from somewhere, to know something intimately as ours. I have forfeited this ancient knowledge for an artificial reality, a virtual reality of schizophrenic experiences that may leave no mark, at least in the physical world. I will never know the place that I am briefly dat-ing in all its moods, all its stages of maturity, all of its hues. I get a snapshot, and that's all I get. Places do become lodged in our body, but only on a microscopic level. I am not attached to them or anything, I float.

I am the stranger icon—I live in oblivion wrestling with nothingness.

But when something is sacrificed, something is always received. I have gained the world, or at least huge swathes of it. I can bridge peoples and lands, I can mediate, I can explain. I am all-seeing, I am global, I am Cubist. I have recreated myself as a three-dimensional being, but one that is simultaneously translucent. Yes, I may have lost my soul in one or more of those places that temporarily claimed me. In those men that remain nameless, faceless, but are also lodged there under my skin. At least I think that's where I left them.

Do they ever think of me the way I do about them? Do they even remember? Do I? We used each other's flesh, and sometimes emotions, for a brief moment in time and space. Was it Teflon, or did it stick? Did we literally slip through each other's arms? Slide right past each other? I want everything to matter, but maybe there are some things that simply don't.

I know, I know, I know, I know—you can't take it with you. There are no souvenirs in life. We're all just passing through. Everything is retreating from us, even the stars. I hate that.

Maybe that's why I've embraced it and taken it in all the way to its extreme—I move through people and places, onwards towards something, some destination I may never get to. There were many glances over my shoulder, many times I thought I should curve my path back around and stay here with this stranger and follow what could (should?) be my new life. But somehow, I didn't. It's ok, I tell myself. Transience is the structure of the world, and there's little you can do to change it.

We can fool ourselves into thinking we're traveling to see, to experience, to meet the man of our dreams, our ultimate reality. But as with most of life, we're probably fooling ourselves. With our eyes on our predetermined prize, the true goal always arises from around our blind sides and comes up to take us over and we never see it coming, ever. The piece of flesh before you is tangible and real and hefty and delicious—and then, like a meal, it's consumed and it's gone.

The flesh is one thing, but the spirit is always attached to the back of it.

Wet Speedos in Puerto Rico

I spotted him in a blue Speedo standing in the waters of the Caribbean. The sea was murky with dark warm waves. The Speedo was light blue, soaking wet and nearly see-through in the sinking sunset. There was a small red label on the right hip and an interior drawstring that was tucked in and didn't show—just a faint outline. The material clung to his brown bulge, visible through two layers of crotch fabric.

This worked for me.

The Speedo fetish I've had since a teenager has granted me the gift for noticing such details. The only erotic outlet available to me as a boy (beyond collecting men's underwear ads, and my own crude stick figure sex drawings) were clandestine stares at my father and his friends lounging around on their boats with nothing covering their adult genitals except thin, flimsy bikini trunks. This was the 1980s. It was a time when hiked-up, narrow, French-cut men's swimsuits were acceptable during some peculiar form of sexual innocence or sexual ignorance. (For those who weren't alive, cross-dressing pop music stars and grown men wearing the color fuschia also occurred during this era of modern history.) My dad's and his pals' bulges jutted on display in a strange macho reversal of outward femininity—in-your-face primal peacock-strutting by way of Spandex. Heavy metal bands of the time followed the same visual philosophy. For a horny, barely-legal gay boy, '80s Lycra was the ultimate gift from the Gods, bulging manna from heaven.

My favorite protuberance of them all was that of the Australian Paul, who wore the skimpiest Speedos of the lot—barely a half-inch of material covering the sides of his tan, muscular hips. Sometimes, the narrow band would slip and I could see how truly white his real skin tone was. I often jacked off picturing what the dark tan lines must look like outlined on his naked body. He owned an array of suits in bright and light colors—the best hues for showing every bump and ridge, I carefully realized. Paul had a bushy mustache and a blond chest that was the living incarnation of my erotic ideal at the time: Tom Selleck in *Magnum P.I.*

One day during the hormone-fueled rage of being fourteen years old, Paul finally caught me gawking—probably salivating—at his manly prominence as he sat with his legs spread in the cockpit of his ketch. I could clearly make out the wide, oblong head of his penis resting peacefully on its side, with the high ridge of its pointed hood, even the fine lines of his soft amber pubic hair, showing through the thin yellow material. Tarzan's stripper loincloth had nothing on this public display of male groin.

But Tarzan was oblivious to his sex appeal, and Paul wasn't. Like the pointy codpieces of the Renaissance, Paul let all passing females know what they could be in for, if they played their cards right. He showed it off to the world, right through his male bikini. When his wife was away, I sometimes witnessed random females disappearing below his deck, following his Speedo pied piper pipe in a hypnotic daze.

I wasn't so lucky. For him, my laser stare on his crotch must have felt like a magnifying glass under direct sunlight. With almost a yelp, he hollered down to his wife below to throw him a pair of shorts. His plea was almost frantic. And here I thought I'd been so coy. The sex-deprived urges of my teenage virginhood stalked this grown man as prey. It was the first time I had power over an adult heterosexual man. His bulge's cockiness was no match for the perverted laser gaze of a young single-minded homosexual.

Later in my twenties, I'd hook up with older guys who kind of looked like Paul, and I'd make them wear Speedos while I fucked them on all fours on the floor.

And now here I was in my thirties, finding myself staring at more Speedo bulges, this time in the warm waves of Puerto Rico. Why exactly I had traveled here, and who I was writing a travel article for, has melted into that hardened lump of past irrelevance. The things we forget, and the visions we remember.

I was staying at a gay beachside hotel called the Atlantic Shores. It was located in Condado, a district just outside of the historical, cobblestone confines of the Old Town of San Juan. It was a place trying hard to be Miami, but it tasted more like margarine than butter. Upscale shops and flashy renovated hotels were trying hard to hide their struggle to overtake the derelict liquor stores and empty shop fronts. It was one of those places halfway through its midlife crisis facelift—street crews courageously attempted to fill in potholes and patch up sidewalks in what appeared to be a losing battle against the mildewed, urban decay of a tropical outpost of America.

It was off-season, and I found myself trapped in the thick humidity of a Caribbean summer, an insect on moist flypaper. Only an odd handful of lost tourists (like myself?) seemed to be eking out the idea of a vacation amid the stained buildings. It was America, but it wasn't. I ate crappy food at Wendy's across the street from the hotel and tried to understand the weird Spanish floating all around me, markedly different from the Mexican-flavored Spanish I grew up around in Southern California.

I ventured out to the gay nightclubs I had found online, located in the grittier Santurce area, a bit of a walk from my hotel. Puerto

Rico was by far the gayest place I'd been to in the Caribbean, and I couldn't leave without having a taste of some of it. I've done it a thousand times—exploring a city's gay underbelly—and it seems that every time it's a chore to push myself out the door. I don't know why. A mixture of retroactive shyness, fear of rejection, laziness, everything. Like I'm eighteen again and anxiously sneaking into my first gay bar. I always press through and am rewarded with a feeling of accomplishment, even if it's never as exciting or interesting as it's supposed to be. I found myself on the balcony of a dark disco, surrounded by strange looks from effeminate young men and scary looks from older heavy men, and me feeling like I had a flashing light on top of my head. No one was unfriendly, and a few drunks tried to strike up awkward chit chat. Everyone spoke English. Some of the Spanish slang I had to translate later: guys calling each other *loca* ("crazy girl") or maricón ("Mary"); *bugarrón y bugarra* (macho straightish guys who fuck gays); *bellaco* (horny); and *bicho* (dick). And my hands-down favorite was the local word for gay—*pato*. It means a duck. Like in the animal. What the hell?

I left the bar, and made the journey back to my hotel. I had heard the beaches in Puerto Rico could be dangerous. And cruisy. Day or night, but especially night. I had read about local gay people being killed on the island, many of them, and in bad ways: burned, decapitated, dismembered. And the police blamed the victims because of their "type of lifestyle." Nothing different from any other state in the U.S., but I knew I had to watch myself either way. Gay sex had only been legal in Puerto Rico since 2005. Sodomite identity on the uber-Catholic isle was all brand new. Even the deep dark corners of the remote Pacific isles I had been to had crossdressers and gayness happily interwoven into their cultures. But one thing I've learned through years of traveling, one languid tropical locale does not equal another. In closeted Puerto Rico, one famously homophobic politician was only outed when a photo surfaced of him bending over to show off his asshole to the world via a gay sex site. His excuse was that he had been working out and wanted to show off his new muscles. Good one!

Near the entrance to my hotel, a macho-looking guy in jeans and a white T-shirt was hanging out at the end of the street, before it hits the sand. He kept staring at me. Was he planning to rip me off? To rape me? I followed his nod and followed him down to the beach. He stood beneath the cement wall, with the streetlight directly over his head, creating a type of dark halo. He pulled out his long, uncut cock. I went up to him. I figured I could yell and someone at the hotel would hear me, at least just before my throat was cut.

He pushed my head down and I smelled his cock. I hate head cheese, and thankfully this smelled fresh. I pulled back the long foreskin, and felt his big cock grow even longer in my mouth, pushing itself away from the back of my throat. It became so long I could barely breathe. I was massaging my cock out of one of the legs of my shorts, and his hairy hand was on the back of my neck. I was trying to suck quickly. Random noises made it seem like there were still some people lingering in the shadows on the beach. All I could see were the city's lights blinking on the waves. He had better cum quick.

The stranger called me *puto*, said something about *leche*, and finally pulled himself out of my eager mouth and sprayed pump after pump of fresh cum all over my forehead and face. It dripped over my eyebrows and into my eyes. He smiled a devilish grin as he watched it spit up all over me. One hand kept my balance on the wall. I was trying not to fall over, like I was being shot at with a gun. My other hand milked each dollop of sperm from his veiny brown shaft. I put my mouth over the cummy head, trying to drink it all down with my throat. That way, I wouldn't have to walk back through the lobby of the hotel and smile to the girl behind the desk with cum stains splattered down the front of my shirt, like a crime scene. Hopefully, I wouldn't have to talk with her or she would probably smell the stranger's huge cumload still on my breath, in the corners of my mouth. I rubbed all the sperm on my forehead into my hair. Hopefully the globs of ejaculate mixed into my hair wouldn't be too obvious.

As I walked down the tiled hallway back to my room, my semi hard-on still flopped around in my loose shorts. I noticed my neighbor's door was open. There were no lights on, but the TV flashed shadows across his bedspread. I could hear the sounds of a bad sitcom laugh track. I peered in. I could see that it was the smiling older Colombian daddy whom I had spoken with briefly in the lobby that morning. He grinned at me, and waved me inside. He pushed back the ugly nylon fire retardant bedspread from his body to reveal that he was completely naked. His thick cock lay to one side, waiting for me. Almost winking at me. I quickly surmised why he had kept his door open, willing himself to stay awake, waiting for me to come home from the bar so I could peer into his door and find him there like this.

His trap worked. I soon found my cock out of my shorts' leg again and myself nursing on my second thick hairy brown cock of the evening. He groaned but said nothing as I pulled back his foreskin and played with his unshaven balls. He shoved his hands down my shorts, and began playing with my asshole. I was glad there was no sand on it from the beach. He pulled out his fingers, spat on them loudly, and shoved them back down my pants. I knew it was going to happen, so I yanked off my shorts, held his thick shaft up to my hole, straddled him on top of the bed, and sat directly on his thick daddy dick. I watched his eyes grow big at the way I was not wasting my time. The taste of the last guy's load in my mouth made me hungry for more cum, it was true. And fucking my next door neighbor was easier and less dangerous than bringing someone home from the bar or the beach. At least that's what I told myself as I pushed up and down on his cock, calling him *papi* until I could feel his dick twitch and swell and fill me up with so much cum that it smeared outside all over my ass cheeks. Like a light switch, his orgasm altered him from horny to instantly embarrassed, and his body nearly recoiled from me. I got the message, pulled on my shorts and left his room, saying *gracias*. Why even be polite? I guess I wanted to leave on a not-too-awkward note. He nodded and ran into his bathroom.

I went back to my room, locked the door, and fingered his fresh cum dripping from my ass. I bent over and looked at my sperm-filled hole in the mirror and jerked off thinking of the two hot loads I had collected in less than a twenty minutes from random strangers who had surfaced in front of me out of the depth of the warm night. I shot all over the floor and let it all dry there as I fell asleep.

I hadn't pulled the blinds shut, so I woke up to a searing blast of sunlight pushing its way through my windows. The room was already stuffy and hot. I pulled myself up naked from the bed and stood at the glass and looked out. Bunches of young people were on the sand, wearing long surfer shorts. Some clumps of overweight lesbians sat underneath palm trees, a mother held her son in the water, and a couple of teenagers (gay? straight?) splashed each other. There were one or two overweight older guys in Speedos. No one looked up at my nude form in the window. The day was already on a full steamroll.

The décor of my "suite" on the third story of the Atlantic Shores Hotel looked like *The Golden Girls*: rickety wicker furniture and faded flower patterns and an idea of the Tropics without the production. I almost felt more comfortable in the time warp of it all, like I had stepped into some old movie of twenty years ago, aged into the present day. I wandered down and joined the random gays sitting on plastic chairs on the hotel's outdoor patio overlooking the beach. The scratchy radio played Shakira over crackling loud-speakers. The unkempt bartender told me how great the Atlantic Shores used to be years ago. How the Sunday tea dances were enormous; how the rooftop used to be a nightclub with the hottest guys; how I should come back in season since it would be better then.

I kind of didn't care. I liked the idea of having the place to myself now, in its decayed form, when you could see it for what it really was. Without makeup on, aging in the bright sunlight, all of its cracks and wrinkles there for everyone to see. Like open wounds. The area would soon be cheerily modernized like everything else in the coming world, and all the texture would be gone. (My premonitions were spot on: Years after my stay, the Atlantic Shores became an upscale straight hotel.)

I went up to the rooftop and could still see where the DJ booth must have played to hot shirtless guys overlooking the cement sky-line all those Sunday afternoons ago. The tiles were dusty and dirty now, and only a cracked plastic chair sat in the corner. Someone had left a cheap paperback book on a table. I picked it up. Some stupid English language romance trying to disguise itself as a real novel. I looked at the copyright. It was over twenty years old. I set it back down, like an artifact that shouldn't be disturbed.

I stared out over the ocean for a while. All the residential high rises levitating up around me, but I could see nothing.

I began to sense the rushed approach of the Puerto Rican sun-set. It fell in a depressing black instant. I had met a Puerto Rican lesbian author in New York City once, and all I can remember from her memoir of the island was the echoing line, "How dark the night is in this place where I was born."

I took the tiny elevator back to the hallway to my room. The Co-lombian daddy's door was shut tight. Earthquakes of jackhammers could be heard a few floors down, where the hotel owners were trying to upgrade something or another before darkness fell. Why bother? It would be easier just to tear the building down, or let it collapse on its own. Let the salt air and blasting sunshine have its way with it. It wouldn't take very long. Just let the past die, honorably. Don't resuscitate it. You wouldn't splash water on a gasping fish dying on a hot sidewalk, would you? You'd step on its head.

The Doors sang on my iPod:
"Tropic corridor
Tropic treasure
What got us this far
To this mild equator?

We need someone or something new
Something else to get us through …"

I couldn't drag myself to another bar, and I couldn't just sit in my room all day. I called my lesbian friend in Florida, and she said I sounded lonely.

I finally logged online to a gay hook up site, and soon found a photo of two beautiful dark brown legs ending inside a well-formed Speedo. I quickly complimented the owner of the legs, and he quickly said thanks, and I quickly suggested we meet on the beach in front of my hotel. Then he paused a great while. I didn't want to beg, but I felt like it. After I sent another compliment or two, he finally relented and told me he lived only a couple blocks away from the hotel and that he'd meet me on the beach wearing the Speedos in the photo.

I galloped downstairs into the rush of the coming sunset. The scratching of my sandals echoed in the stairway. I waited, afraid I'd bump into the questioning white T-shirt daddy I had sucked off here the night before, but in the stark truth-telling light of day.

I waited on my towel, trying to suck in my stomach, trying to pose casually in my Speedos on one arm, trying not to feel like a fool or even care about a stranger I'd never met before. I tried to be inconspicuous.

I scanned the sand for a while as the light kept dying in front of my eyes. I finally saw a jet-black-haired man waist-deep in the waves. I waited for the water to retreat around his groin, and there it was—the same light blue Speedo I had seen on the Internet.

His body was muscular, beefy, and smooth. And well-proportioned, like a careful drawing. He was short, clean shaven, and very handsome. On cue, the setting rays of light dipped behind some clouds. The soft, diffused light gave him the aura of an aqua dream, a Botticelli male Venus rising out of the Caribbean sea.

I lost my inhibitions as I heeded the Siren's call. I waded into the water wearing my own black Speedo. I smiled, and he knew it was me. I took him further out into the water, and hugged his wet, hairless body. We began to kiss, and I was surprised he was so open about our sudden entanglement, he being a guy from the neighborhood and all. Anywhere one goes in the world, tourists are easy, anonymous prey for locals. Just as long as your friends don't see.

The sticky saltwater embraced us, forming a kind of cocoon around us. The sun sank into the ocean, and we trudged back out of the water, trying to hide our erections in our clingy swimsuits.

He was a lawyer, nearly forty (although looking ten years younger in that Latin way that makes me so envious). He didn't smile much, even when I tried to make some lame jokes. But when he did smile, it lit up the whole beach. He was smart, coy.

"Can I take you out to dinner sometime?" I heard myself saying. Why did I say that before I had him naked? He just smiled and laughed. I'm the last person to offer a date after a first kiss on the beach, but I simply wanted to spend more time in his presence. A vision flashed in my mind of me back on the island on some future trip and sitting on the beach and laughing and kissing him in the salty, dark waves.

After a quick visit to my suite (the management says no guests allowed upstairs, but I somehow escorted him up without a hitch), he pulled down his damp trunks, and I liked seeing them in a wet heap on my tiled floor. He lay back on the bed, I tasted the salt on his body, and suddenly it seemed to be over. I know he came, but I don't know how. All my memory recalls is his damp trunks going back on and him down the hall and vanishing back into the wall of high rises behind me. I ate dinner alone that night, I forget where.

I emailed him again, called him even, trying to sound casual and good-natured on his voicemail. I walked the empty beach at night, staying in the streetlights and away from any strange outlines moving towards me.

The Doors continued on my iPod:
"When all else fails
We can whip the horse's eyes
And make them sleep
And cry ..."

I never heard from him. My Venus had faded away as quickly as he had appeared. Maybe back into the sea where he had originally come from. Maybe another night with him would have made him too human, too flesh and blood. Maybe it was better I was alone now. Maybe that was all I needed from him.

Now he would remain my fantasy—and never my reality.

Seeing Red in Estonia

He had a light red mustache above his pink lips, and was eyeing me from a park bench. He was about my same age at the time, in his early twenties, and I was taken aback by how incisive his stare was. His hair was so red it looked like it was dyed, but it wasn't. A splatter of freckles made sexy constellations across his face.

Full disclosure: Redheads are my least favorite flavor of men. I know, it sounds racist or something. White-on-white prejudice. But you must understand that my two siblings are both redheads. My brother and my sister looked like twins, but weren't. But that didn't keep them from being hired as such in modeling and acting gigs. They appeared in all kinds of TV commercials and print ads before their puberty put an end to their marketable red cuteness. (Redheads don't age well—there, I said it.)

I tried out for ads too—but never got even one. That's because I was brown-haired, like most of the planet's population. Sure, I had their same dimples and freckles, but I knew I couldn't compete with the Caucasian genetic quirk that both our grandfathers had had as well, and had passed down to my brother and sister but somehow forgot me. My two redhead siblings knew they were superior because they stood out as different—not freaks, but simply unique and striking. And they knew this because people paid them money for it. I was generic, I faded into the woodwork of brownness.

Does that sound like a chip on my shoulder? You bet it does.

But this redhead on the park bench was sexy. I hated to admit it to myself, but I was attracted to him. For the first time in my life I had that thought about anyone who even remotely looked like my own siblings. The boy's hair was bright red and straight and his freckles seemed to glow on his ultra-white face like neon dots. Normally, that would totally turn me off. But I guess he was just foreign enough—and horny enough—to get past my biased radar.

I had just climbed down the limestone hill where the thirteenth-century Toompea Castle imposes itself over the little winding city of Tallinn, in the Baltic country of Estonia. It was the beginning of fall, the leaves were quickly turning brown—and, appropriately, bright red—in anticipation of a horrible, dark Russian-fed winter.

The redhead's eyes would not let go of me. His red eyelashes didn't even seem to blink as he drank me in. So I strolled up to his park bench and, with a charming American smile, asked him if he spoke English. He shook his head. *Parle russki?* Another no. *Parle francais?* No. *Habla espanol?* No. I was running out of languages I barely spoke, but all I could do was stand there before his smiling, dancing eyes. They said yes.

"You," I pointed with a finger, "Estonia?" I pointed to the ground.

He looked at me, and then my finger, and then nodded.

"Mama, papa, Estonia?" figuring everyone knows those words. Another nod and smile. His teeth were whiter than white under his silly little mustache.

I brought my cupped hand to my mouth in a drinking motion. "Drink?"

He nodded and said something that evidently meant *sure*, and we were on our way across the cobblestone streets of Tallinn's old town. Crumbling old buildings and women with head scarves passed us by, as he lead me to a little cellar bar that had wooden tables and candles. I had already checked, and there were no gay bars or gay anything in Estonia. But I guess he knew we'd be okay here.

The redhead and I somehow kept our non-conversation going there, over cups of hot spiced wine and candlelight. He looked around every now and then, Tallinn being a small town and all and he being with this English-speaking foreigner doing God knew what. I telegraphed the fact that I was from America, that I had just been to Russia before coming to Estonia, and I would be going to Finland next. By using place names and lots of Italian-quality hand movements, I got across the overall idea of what I was saying. I found out he was going to university (opened palms like a book meant school, we discovered), and that he lived outside of town with his family (a sweeping motion with his arm and those valuable words mama and papa). He didn't drive (fists on an invisible steering wheel), didn't smoke (two fingers to the lips), and, if the fact needed to be hammered home any further, he only spoke Estonian. To me, it was a weird language. Even though it is related to Finnish, it sounded like Spanish to my ears for some reason.

The fact we had no common language didn't seem to really matter in our pursuit of one another. We were both young, alone, gay, and horny. It was all so obvious, even without any definite words. Our clandestine park pick-up was like an unspoken secret between the two of us.

I dragged the redhead back to the large room I was renting in a local family's apartment. The corpulent mother was friendly and the only one in the house who spoke English.

"Are you also from America?" she asked my new friend, wondering why we were hurrying up the stairs to my room.

"He's from here," I explained over my shoulder, casually, like me and the red head were old buddies. The mother and he exchanged a few words in Estonian, and she tried to smile it all away. I'm sure she was wondering who the hell I was taking back to her house, and what we had planned to do there.

We got into my room, and suddenly we were on the floor, kissing so hard one of us could have busted a lip. We began wrestling on the old knitted rug, trying not to make any noise. But we were like wild dogs let loose inside the house. When we knocked over a small table, the mother knocked on the door. "Is everything ok in there?"

"Yes, fine." I replied through the locked door, and the redhead giggled softly.

We still had our clothes on, and I began to slowly peel them off of him, holding my finger to my lips the whole time for him to keep quiet. His flesh was so white, it looked like it had never seen sunshine, ever. The pink undertones to his skin, and the playful freckles, like a bashful rash, sparkled with life. I finally pulled his underwear off, and a long and fleshy peach-colored cock bounced out at my face. It was framed by a fire bush of almost incandescent burnt orange pubic hairs. I thought this would repel me, like the few times I showered with my brother's bright bush staring at me. But instead, I was intrigued. It was a new flavor of ice cream I had never tasted. His foreskin was so long it dangled off the end of his dick, giving it another good inch. I pulled it back to make sure it was clean, and was welcomed with a bright pink head staring at me with a huge wide piss slit, already oozing happy precum. I sucked it until it spat all over my face in a robust response.

He being the young lad he was, it didn't go down after he shot his wad. And he didn't either. He roughly impaled his mouth on my cock and then forced it into his pink anus, with barely any spit for lube. He didn't care. He wanted to take a ride on America, and I would not begrudge him. He kept making primal grunting noises that sounded like something humans did even before languages were invented. I had to put my hand over his mouth to keep him quiet.

The sex was so good, his eyes so intense and alive, his touch so genuine. I didn't want him to go, so we had another hand-gesture meal that evening and then met again in the dark red autumn daylight and walked around the town. I moved into a cheap hotel around the corner since the mother was catching on to our shenanigans, and I ended up spending nearly a week with my Estonian redhead. We'd roll around the starched white sheets of the tiny hotel bed at night, kissing deeply like old lovers and then sit next to each other in cafés during the day like inseparable school chums. And we never spoke a word to each other.

Somehow, we were never bored or awkward with each other. We never ran out of things to gesture about. We had an unspoken mutual language, the redhead and I, and I'm not exactly sure what it was. Perhaps something unfathomable and transcendental that naked men sleeping in each other's arms have been speaking between each other for centuries, or eons.

A Vegas Losing Streak

After spotting him at the gym earlier that afternoon, I bumped into him again at a dark, empty bar down from The Strip. It was one of those places far from the giddy, hyper neon, where only die-hard or desperate gay tourists to Vegas find the desert wind blowing them to. Newspapers in the street.

I forgot how I had wound up there.

Vegas' gay life is there, hidden and huddled around a strip of honky tonk bars lovingly called "The Fruit Loop." Visitors rarely find the area, and when they do, they show up before midnight like the true amateurs they are. No one is there. Locals have no sense of night versus day or real money versus play money. The lights extend from the bars on to the concrete and into the vanishing desert night and all the way until they meet oblivion. For all the fabulousness and over-the-topness and sequins and colored lights and cartoon monuments and promises to keep, garish Vegas has no sense of gayness.

The bartender promises me there'll be hot guys there later. Promises: the fuel that Vegas runs on.

I had already had a couple drinks and was bold enough to waltz right up to my gym flirt from earlier in the day. He was at the bar, poised at the open door and the wind and newspapers outside and he teetered, like he wasn't sure if gravity would be pushing him further in or sucking him back out. I was close to his face, where I could smell the alcohol on his breath. His smile was almost boy-like at my tipsy attempts to be charming. He was smooth, milky white, in his forties with a circular, firm, pumped-up body and a protruding backside. I was the younger one, but he was my prey.

He had ended up here, empty-handed after his romantic gam-bles of the evening. He had been ready to cash in his chips and accept his losses for the night, but he didn't know when to leave. Then I had appeared, a roulette wheel that suddenly turned in his favor. He hoped. I was the new promise.

"C'mon, let's go back to the bed and breakfast I'm staying at," I ordered. He quickly agreed. Did he have a choice in the matter?

He sprawled out across the field of my bed like a dry harvest. He was round and firm and hairless and his cock was so white it almost glowed in the dark. His skin was rubbery in a sexy way. If I looked closely enough, I might be able to see through it to blue veins pumping real blood that would be going somewhere. His small boyish dick was surrounded by a few pubes that were almost white. His legs were thick and meaty up on my shoulders, as I tried to haul them up above me like lumber.

He was going through some unspoken, prescribed motions of not accepting loss for loss's sake. He would not give in to his pre-vious bad luck of the evening. He was obdurate. He let me do all the work, like I was the one who had hit the jackpot. It was physi-cal labor. We were both following a standard recipe someone had written for us a long time ago. Somehow pleasure would sponta-neously arise between us, and hopefully it wouldn't then promptly collapse under its own weight like a soufflé.

But the thin night collapsed around us regardless.

We soon heard an enormous breaking of glass. Not like a cup or two had fallen, but rather like a whole patio door had exploded and burst into the house. He jumped up in my bed, as if he had been zapped with a cattle prod. I could make out the whites of his eyes in the dark. "What the hell was that?"

"I'll go check, stay here," I commanded like a knight. Armored in a towel wrapped around my waist, I ventured out into the large ranch house cum gay bed and breakfast. We were deep in the nameless, faceless suburbs of Vegas, the areas the tourism board doesn't want you to find and where noise is rare.

I heard voices and peeked through a crack in the door of the TV room. The two British owners of the B&B were standing apart from each other. Swaying. Eyeing each other like cowboys at a duel. A large and completely obliterated glass table lay between them, creating a lake of cracked crystal on the carpet.

I bravely slid open the door. "Is everything okay?"

They barely looked at me. One began howling at the other. "Look what you've done, you fuck up!"

"Fuck you! You're stinking drunk!" It was then that the other one stooped down to pick up a shard of the glass table and pointed it at the less drunk one. A trickle of blood made its way down his hand.

I strode forward in my towel and caught his arm. "C'mon, drop the glass. You," I turned to the other, "get into the kitchen." Like everyone that night, they did as I commanded.

After many tears, swabbing of red glass cuts, and trying to snatch the car keys away from the drunk one before he zoomed off (which he did anyway), I realized my damsel in distress back in my other room was long gone. He had somehow pulled on his clothes and thrown out a hasty goodbye to me through all the commotion.

His losing streak had not ended that night, after all.

But he was a smarter gambler than me. He knew when to leave the game. I stayed up all night pouring coffee and handing over pieces of Kleenex, the doctor of the Dysfunctional Gay B&B.

The next morning I took a cue from my late-night guests and bee-lined it to the door, but not before the now-sober owner charged me the full price for my stay. I stood at his computer as he slowly and carefully printed out my receipt, which was not cheap. I just wanted to get out of there, to forget, to pretend I wasn't calculating my own losses in front of a stranger. Who owes who in life anyway? Thank God we don't hand each other bills on a regular basis—we'd all be in debt.

I zoomed away in my stupid rental car, towards the asylum of a neutral airport. The towers and spires and fairy-tale guarantees of The Strip laughed at me, giants in a row. I could do nothing but hold my head down and take it.

I heard later that the B&B had closed down, not surprisingly. I guess losses happen all the time in Vegas. And the ones that come out of your wallet are the least risky of them all.

The Senegalese Air Conditioner Boy

Outside my room, the boy looked up at me with piercing yet puppy-dog eyes. He was bent over an air-conditioner unit, the arid African sunshine beating down on his sweaty brow. He had on shorts and a tight T-shirt and was on his haunches working alongside another man. Although I'm used to being stared at as the token whitey in many countries, this boy's gaze seemed to last a few sexual beats too long.

When I returned later, he was still there outside my hotel room door, even sweatier and nearly done with his work on the air conditioner. His gaze seemed even more intent this time, like he was trying to see through me, like my white skin could be translucent if you looked hard enough. I went over and struck up some inane conversation in my crappy high school French. He just smiled and nodded and answered back in his heavy Senegalese French. I loved the depth and valleys of his voice, coming from a thin but masculine twenty-something young man.

"Do you want to go for a walk around the village later?" he invited. I agreed, and around dusk he picked me up at my room in a fresh pair of tight jeans and we sauntered around his tiny hamlet. It was like a date of some sort. The streets were all hard dirt, and fluorescent lights and lanterns flickered in open windows as African pop music floated about. I had been to Africa enough times to know that my newfound friend was amiable and innocent. And horny.

We stopped at his house, and I gingerly met his parents and siblings who were watching a Muslim sermon on a TV sitting in the front yard. We sat there for a long while in this open-air living room, with a cat stretching on its side on the cement and a kid or two playing with their fingernails and the parents trying to stay awake, quiet in the thick air. The night was bone-dry and warm and dusty and restless. We were light years away from any bright cities, and the dark sky shone above. The five calls to prayer for the day were long over, and they sat and listened to the cleric on TV go on and on and on.

It was my third trip to West Africa. Once again, I was home. More here than I ever was in my own country. Funny how that happens. I always felt bad for people who didn't travel, who never knew where they really belonged.

The dry winds of the Sahel—that weird strip of dotted Africa just before the sandy sea of the Sahara completely takes over the continent—they blow for hundreds of miles all around. All the way through the streets of Dakar, the capital of Senegal. I had already been to its cafés, watched its rather stuck-up ladies prance around in their bright African mumus and matching headdresses, visited the stomach-churning slave fortresses of Gorée Island with its loading docks for human cattle. The pastel colonial edifice of the slave prison, the abode to so much indescribable pain, looked bright and nearly cheerful in the insistent Senegalese sunshine. "It's a hard history," my guide had simply said.

My guide also told me not to tell anyone he had helped translate an interview with a local gay leader for me. "I am not one of them, I don't want to be," he insisted with a stern look.

For an article I was writing on gay life in Africa, I had tracked down the soft-spoken twenty-six-year-old president of Andligeey (who didn't want his name published). We spoke over dinner in a Dakar restaurant. My guide sat between us, he was not happy at all. The activist was small and slight. I paid for dinner, and he was happy. The guide couldn't wait to get out of there—he had to sit through the activist telling me how gay sex is illegal but very common for married men here and how local gays have been arrested at beaches, at private homes, and once at a private "gay wedding." In theory, Senegal is one of the most tolerant Muslim societies on Earth, with wide religious freedoms, a taste for sexy fashions, and even legalized prostitution. But when Senegal's first gay organization Groupe Andligeey (translated as "Walking Together") tried to arrange a meeting of some of its 400 members at a Dakar hotel, Senegal's Interior Ministry immediately moved to prevent the gathering "so that such a demonstration is not organized on national territory."

I had seen French tourists lounging around topless at the closed-off Club Med south of Dakar, at the touristy hetero resort land of La Petite Côte ("The Little Coast"), ignorant to any of this going on.

My little thin activist still pressed me to write to encourage gay and lesbian tourists to come to Senegal. "It's the only way for people to understand that there are two very different gay worlds: the one in the Western world and the one in developing countries," my unhappy guide translated, nearly rolling his eyes.

A year later, I got an email from the activist saying he had fled Senegal and become a refugee in France. More arrests had occurred and he was not safe in Senegal any longer. A poll had shown that 96% of Senegalese thought homosexuality should be rejected by society, and more gays had been thrown in jail since I'd visited.

It wasn't an AIDS-backlash. Less than 5% of Senegal's population is HIV+ and the government has been proactive about AIDS education and blood screening. And most HIV cases in Africa are heterosexual anyway. It probably had more to with the die-hard Muslin imams and local leaders who stoked the anti-gay fires, just like the die-hard Jewish leaders do in Israel and the die-hard Christians do in the U.S. It seemed to me a long way from what I researched about the gay-accepting Senegal of pre-colonial times, when the Wolof tribe had "men-women" called *gor-digen* and when musical storytellers called *griots* were outwardly "gay." European visitors even wrote about boy brothels near Dakar as late as the 1950s. Maybe globalization and media brought too much to Africa after all. It couldn't live in its own bubble anymore.

That night, after a sitting and watching the imam on TV for a long spell, me and my air conditioner boy finally left his parents. We strolled together on our little date, but I didn't dare touch him in public where his village could see him. He didn't talk much, and I followed suit. We sauntered to the local tailor shop, run by another young man. He had good English and wore a flashy-patterned shirt. It hung down over his baggy pants, and I'm sure he made his own clothes, but they were good. The tailor's face lit up when I entered the small brick room. There was no glass covering the window holes in the walls, and a tin shed created the ceiling.

"Ah, you are from America, everything is very free there," he intimated with a wink. He kept looking at me and the air conditioner boy, smiling. He seemed to be the smartest kid in town. Another somewhat effeminate young man appeared in another shirt with flashy patterns, and I quickly realized that in this microscopic hamlet in deep dusty Senegal, this was the gay gathering spot. Smiles and nods and oblique understanding transcended all distance between us, like we all shared some common queer ancestor in our genetic trees.

After the homosexual tailor shop, we seemed to be finished with the village's social screening process. I got the feeling my friend was trapped by the minuscule village and its muted way of life, and that I was a fascinating flashlight from another world shining in front of him. He led me to a small, empty pier at the edge of town. We were finally alone.

The jetty silently jutted out into the warm Atlantic. Cricket chirps and the low, nearly unheard drum beats of the continent created a wall of sound behind us. I put my hand on his shoulder and squeezed it. He quickly grabbed me and pressed his lips hard against mine, like he was trying to breathe in something. He fumbled with his clothes and mine, in a frantic race against the falling night. I pushed his tight jeans down and threw my head on his small cut cock. He held my skull like a vice with both of his calloused hands. I turned him around and held him tight in my arms and pressed my perfectly rigid dick against his hard, dark buttocks. They had little coils of hair on them that tickled my naked shaft. He grated up against me, pushing his body back into mine. I didn't get inside him, I wanted to, but he came quickly and ecstatically, shooting his seed far across the pier, finally expelling something he had bottled up inside, with a type of anger and relief and excitement a small-town gay anywhere in the world would tacitly comprehend.

On the way home I took a picture of him and we exchanged email addresses. I handed him a small *cadeau* of a few dollars. In Africa, one always gives gifts regardless of the circumstances, and this was far from prostitution on his part. In fact, the dark night of Africa had given me a gift of understanding how important a foreign stranger's presence can be for the remote and exiled of the world.

Making Love Not War in Russia

I t was just right after Soviet Communism had given its last hur-
rah and puttered out into the hazy rear view mirror of history.
This was way before oil and Gucci and Pucci had flushed their
way through the country. This was when alcoholism and bitterness were the tsars of the land—when the acidic resentfulness of
having been fed a century of proletariat lies was still fresh in everyone's mouths. They had lost the war, and they knew it. There was
a tangible darkness to the place, all around the edges and creeping
inward, like chaos was in charge and nobody else.

Kids roamed the streets in packs and grabbed the banana I was
munching on (bananas having been a recently-introduced luxury
item in the new Russia). I flung the rest of the peel directly at them,
and the urchins roared with laughter. I had heard they surround
foreigners in packs and pick their pockets. They would always
survive. I had also heard an American couple had been murdered
inside their hotel room in Moscow. Later, I saw an elderly man in
a hat get violently mugged across the street from me, screaming
and begging for help. There were no taxis in that Russia—you just
waved your arms on the side of the road and, for a few rubles,
someone would stop to take you where you wanted to go. But there
were dark stories of passengers being taken to the countryside and
robbed and left there.

The Russian mafia, casually ostentatious in their black limos and shiny Italian suits, seemed to be the only ones enjoying themselves and offering any kind of structure to reality. They were the symbol of safety and stability rather than dread and fear. They operated all the nice restaurants, where an excess of under-employed uniformed attendants just stood around, wondering what to do, wondering what capitalism was all about.

St. Petersburg was the only time I had been thrown out of a public place. And this place was very public. A public human carwash of sorts, right next to one of the city's main train stations. It was in an old, stained, single-story building, once ornate but now ramshackle. I found it through my trusty *Spartacus* guide. A few rubles got you in, an attendant locked away your belongings, you were handed a bar of cheap soap and a flimsy towel, and then you made your way into the men's side of the building. It was like a gay bathhouse, but for the everyman. No one checked your sexuality here. Communism had meant lack of plumbing in houses, and men simply came here to shower, gossip, sauna, shower again, and get away from their wives. And with the lack of anything overtly gay at the time in the newly-collapsed U.S.S.R., these public baths were also the de facto homo hangouts as well.

I roamed around the place, getting my bearings the exact way I would at a gay bathhouse. There were several rows of individual shower stalls, none of them with curtains. Steam rose all around and made the air humid. In the back, there was a large dry wooden sauna with three levels of seating in it, like a mini-coliseum. Completely naked men took turns whacking each other with birch leaves while the others looked on indifferently. The room was rank with the perspiration of fat and/or ugly men, only broken by the springtime stench of birch bits flying about everywhere. When I exited the sauna, I had to pick off the green leaves stuck to my white skin. A few sideways glances, but I really couldn't tell if anyone was cruising the way the guidebook had prophesized. It's so hard sometimes to read a foreign culture—I sensed they knew I wasn't Russian, even without my telltale Western clothing on. Maybe that's why they stared at me. *What was this weird naked American kid doing in here anyway?*

I spied into the shower stalls as I passed them, and sometimes I would spot a guy's hands linger around his groin a little longer than need be. I planted myself across the row from one of these crotch cleaners—a hot hairy tall guy with a receding hairline. I gingerly became erect as I showered, acting like I didn't notice my own hard-on, slowly turning this way and that like a watery rotisserie. Oh, how I love to show off sometimes—especially fully naked in public, with barely a thin towel to retreat to. Receding Hairline Bather watched my display and began methodically jerking himself off, like a masturbatory robot. I started to make my way out of my stall into his, but his hand went up to stop me. I withdrew back into my booth and gazed intently as he ejaculated all over his wall. The creamy bits of wasted sperm slowly dripped their way down from the wall, making their languid way into the drain to mix with the rest of the dark city's refuse.

On another round through the stalls, I spotted an enthusiastic shower stall inhabitant who stared straight at me. He had a little chair in there with him and kept bending over it, rubbing suds all over his ample, hairless, wet buttocks. He had a mustache—most men in Russia hadn't got the memo that facial hair had long since gone extinct in most parts of the world. I watched as he fingered his hole, beckoning for me to join him. I had brought in a couple condoms with me and picked one up and rolled it over my hard cock. I walked towards him. He looked at me quizzically. Rubbers were another luxury item they hadn't seen too much of in Russia.

I sat on his chair and watched as his huge ass rode my pink cock, hot water cascading all around us. I kept an eye out, as there was one tall mustached attendant who regularly made the rounds among the stalls, turning off dripping water and straightening things up. Mustache Big Ass kept riding my condomed cock, not seeming to mind that we only had soap for lube. I finally shot a huge load in the latex, and he groaned. I pulled out, grabbing the base of the condom, and ran over back to my stall.

Just at that exact moment, the attendant walked down my row, looking surlier than ever. He took one glance down at my hands trying to cover up my condom cock. He could see the tip was filled with cum. He yelled—screamed—something in Russian and made a backwards jerking gesture with his hand. I got the message. I sprinted naked to my stall and grabbed at my towel, as he continued to yell at me. Another attendant threw my clothing at me, and I could feel the whole place stopping and staring at me. I haphazardly put my clothes on and darted out of the place. My hair was wet, and there was still soap on my back, but I didn't care. I looked behind me. I was safe. I had escaped. I kept walking as fast as I could. I needed to get out of this city before the police threw my perverted ass in jail.

And luckily, I had a get away plan. I had a train to catch.

It was getting dark, and I ran into the train station to board the night train to Tallinn, my backpack wrapped around me like a protective shield. I held a train ticket in my outstretched hand, unsure if I had even bought the correct one at the window. I piled into my numbered compartment. There were three other men inside. I quickly snuggled into my designated sleeper berth. But just before the train was revving up to leave, a businessman entered the compartment and politely informed me in perfect English, "I believe you are in my berth."

"I am?"

We compared tickets, and he pointed out that my ticket's date was wrong. It was for tomorrow night. I felt the train begin to pull out of the station. How would they throw me off? Just wait to pull out of the station and then chuck my bag on to the dark steppes and my body after it? Would the police be there, waiting to send me to Siberia and to a salt mine for public fornicators?

The businessman sensed my terror and calmly suggested, "If you give the conductor five dollars, I'm sure he can find a place for you." In the chaos of Russia, money talked, bullshit walked. Especially American money and American bullshit.

I spotted the back of a conductor's jacket making its way down the narrow passageway. I tapped the shoulder, and the uniform turned around. Standing in front of me was a tall, twenty-something man with gleaming eyes, a gorgeous smile, and a muscular frame bursting out of his tight jacket. Sand-colored hair tousled out from under his cute quasi-military cap. It was like a bad porno, with accents even and uniforms. I was in lust.

I fumbled for a five-dollar bill in my pocket and followed him down the dark hallway like a stray puppy. He smiled and slid open a rickety compartment door. He indicated that this was where I would be sleeping. It was a Spartan section with four bunk-bed berths housed under flickering fluorescent lights. Two of the beds had other train workers sprawled all over them. They smiled.

Instantly, a bottle of vodka magically appeared, as well as a small table full of shot glasses. And slices of thick salami. Before I knew it, I was downing generic-label vodka shots with my new compartment buddies. Each slug was followed by a delicious, fatty chunk of meat, God knew from what kind of animal. Only one of my bunk mates spoke any semblance of English. "Wisconsin," he kept telling me. "I was in Wisconsin."

They loved their new compartment companion, this strange creature from another world, the so-called Free World. A creature that would have been unimaginable in their presence just a few years earlier.

I found out through Wisconsin Boy that Sandy Hair Conductor was named Sasha, and he didn't speak a lick of English. Was it me getting wasted, or was each vodka shot inching Sasha closer to my body on the tiny bed? He leaned back on to my leg and held his firm torso there. His back muscles were like steel, the bones in his body like lead. He was like a Terminator—a hot, fleshy, Russian Terminator. I began to carefully, minutely stroke his skin through his starched uniform. Sasha the Terminator didn't recoil. In fact, his firm but yielding flesh seemed to push back harder against me.

The others began to pass out like flies, falling into rhythmic snoring. Sasha stood up and put his tight jacket and cute little hat back on. He bent down, kissed me right on the lips and gestured with the hunks of flesh that were his hands that he had to make the rounds around the train and would be right back for me.

I must have passed out too, since I was suddenly awoken by a shirtless Sasha unbuttoning my jeans. I glanced up to the berth across from us, but all I could see was someone's comatose arm dangling from above, bouncing along with the movement of the train like it was dribbling a basketball. Sasha judo-flipped me over so that I was on top of his burly frame. (He seemed to have some experience moving bodies around these cramped spaces.) His two hard and juicy golden buttocks jumped up at me, calling me, egging me on, defying me. I fumbled for the last condom in my bag, spat in my hand, and the train chugged and heaved, the dark landscape of Russia rushing by us in a frenzy, like an X-rated Sergei Eisenstein cinematic montage. I pumped and pumped his huge, hard ass, and he drilled it back onto me, almost pushing me into the wall. His ass needed pumping, and needed it bad. I was only happy to oblige. It was détente, and I was so glad the Cold War was over and America could finally, ultimately, triumphantly invade Russia—and Russia loved it.

The next morning, the other train workers stirred in their hungover stupor, and Sasha escorted me onto the platform, where he scrawled down his address for me. I searched and searched for over a week, but I never found his home.

Trains pass in the night and reach their destinations and you never get back on them and they vaporize over the horizon and the dark steppes swallow them whole. Every now and then, badly accented porn percolates up and becomes alive in everyday reality and then sputters out like a videotape getting eaten in an old VCR.

Moving quickly in the darkness, fantasies and memories are soul mates, after all.

Skin on Skin at an Australian Beach

L ast week a crocodile nearly ate a lady's dog as she was walking along this beach," the man leaning against a pine tree said to me. He had a baggy red tank top on and no pants. The dark tip of his penis bobbed out from underneath the hem of the shirt, which flapped lazily in the salt breeze. His bare feet stood in a bed of pine needles. The shallow surf pounded away impatiently at the long, flat, hard sand in front of us.

"But the tail of the croc splashed in the water and the little dog got away by a hair." He giggled deeply, with an ironic humor that can only be termed *Australian*. "Most dogs around here aren't so lucky!"

All I had heard about since I arrived in Darwin was news about crocodile attacks—a dog here, an elderly man there, a twelve-year-old girl who leaped into a billabong pond never to be seen again. It added an unsettling, primordial edge to the otherwise sleepy and languid town. The people here were kind and innocuous—it was the scenery itself you needed to keep an eye on.

The pantless man handed me a cigarette. He lit it for me as the moist breeze half-heartedly tried to put it out. He stood there casually in his shirt. His penis didn't grow and push up on the hem the way I was expecting. Maybe he was straight. Maybe he was a real nudist. With a shirt on?

I stood there. At least I was completely naked, with just sandals on. I could feel the other stranger's semen still inside me. I didn't have to worry about it dripping out, it was in there very deep. It still felt warm. And salty.

Me and my new friend stood there and looked out on to the calm, neon waters of the Timor Sea. We were so far north in Australia that Indonesia was much closer to us than Sydney. It's a part of Australia so little populated and far-flung and forgotten, it's not even a state—it's just simply The Northern Territories. What could sound more blank on a map than that? You could see that Darwin (the territory's capital named after the evolutionist) was in the midst of tarting herself up with a swanky little hotel there, a classy little restaurant there. But Darwin was a remote and sluggish tropical outpost of just 130,000 souls, and there was no getting around it. Aboriginal women sat in the parks under the shade of flowering trees and watched their kids run around. And even they seemed to run in slow motion, like a cartoon flip book. The Japanese had bombed the place something like fifty times during World War II, but I pictured the bombs kind of floating down through the hot air in zigzags, like leaves.

During my teenage years, I had spent some time on the other side of the Timor Sea, in the island nation of Papua New Guinea. That place was even slower—it didn't even have television when my family and I lived there. We were on my dad's sailboat, anchored at a moldy old Australian navy base that had been given back to the Papuans upon independence. I was fifteen years old, and I was lucky enough to be allowed to use the same showers the guys on the base used. There were only a few soldiers stationed here, but if I hit the timing right I could stand under the water in the communal showers and gaze upon completely naked grown men with suds cascading over their jet black Melanesian skin, getting caught in their curly body hair on the way down. The men had short, muscular, tight bodies, and it was heaven.

I had to wear underwear when I showered. It wasn't out of modesty—I was already quite the exhibitionist at that age. It was because if I didn't wear the tightest pair of underwear I could find, I would have been standing there with a lily white hard-on jutting directly out from my boy body. And anyone—even my dad—could have walked into the bathrooms and seen it. Rather than try to hide my perpetual erection, I realized it was safer to just grab whatever clandestine glances I could. I figured out if I sat in the last bathroom stall, I could look through the crack in the door and spy on the showers that way. Once, when I was staring at a lone dude showering, taking his time soaping himself, I jacked off and shot the biggest wad all over the back of the stall door. It landed with a thud on the cement floor, and I could have sworn he turned around because of the noise the thud. Oh, if only one of the men had gotten hard too, or had come on to me, oh what could have happened …

The half-naked man standing in front of me on the beach in Darwin was Aborigine, not Melanesian. He had more a lanky, angular body, like a runner's. As a connoisseur of all the world's flavors of men, I knew the difference. But he was close enough to my childhood objects of masturbation. His curly body hair and gorgeous dark skin brought back memories. We were in an area just outside of Darwin called Casuarina Free Beach—"Free" because it was the city's one officially clothing-optional strip of sand, marked as such on either end by two tall pillars that looked like striped barber's poles. With only a once-a-night gay pub in town, I had guessed that only pretty much gay or bi-curious men were scattered along the huge beach, seeking any kind of sex they could get their hands on. But straight men need to get off as well, God only knows, and they probably ventured here too. There were no buildings in sight, only a green-blue ocean that spread on forever, teeming with poisonous box jellyfish and saltwater crocs ("salties"). A twisted maze of mangroves lined the back of Casuarina Free Beach, and I assumed these were full of crocodiles lying in wait for sweet humans to lunch on too.

"This beach is so pretty and quiet, I'd never guess people get attacked by wild animals here," I remarked to my pantless friend.

He chuckled again, casually drawing on his cigarette. "Most people can outrun a croc, so it never worries me too much." He smiled a crooked grin. "Do you wanna go back and look at the mangroves? It's low tide, so we don't have to worry about crocs there."

I knew he had more than crocs on his mind as he gazed at my exposed ass. He seemed animal, like he could smell the sperm up in there that I was trying to hide. The load had cum from an older gray-haired white guy further down the beach. He was lying naked on a blanket. As I slowly strolled down the beach buck naked, I kept glancing at him and saw his long dick grow more and more upright until it was pointing straight to the cloudless sky. I went up to him, got down on my hands and knees and put it in my mouth, tasting his river of precum. Then, without asking permission, I lowered my bare butt directly on to it until it was all the way inside of me. The man's eyes shut tight in pleasure, as a lot of men's do when they feel themselves deep within me. They go into another world, and they tell me my ass feels incredible. I don't know how it feels different from any other ass, but it always gets men off quickly. And I like that—knowing that it feels so good that they can't hold back and just need to erupt inside of it. Like I am doing them a service they need.

I sat on my haunches, my feet on the ground, with the older man completely inside me, the hair of my buttocks brushing up on his pubic hair. Then told him—ordered him, I guess—to cum inside of me.

"It won't take long," was all he said before I felt spurt after spurt of his long dick empty its white sperm inside me. I pushed myself further down onto his almost wooden cock, making sure it got deposited deep. Not a drop fell out when I lifted myself off of him. I noticed his wedding ring, but even without it, I could tell he was a father and husband and possibly even a grandfather and I had done him a great favor by relieving him. I smiled as I walked away, his warmth inside of me. My cock was erect, bouncing in the breeze. I was so turned on thinking how we had barely exchanged words, how it was all primal and physical, the deep physical needs men have.

But feeling a stranger's sperm in me only makes my ass hungrier. I hate the feeling of needing more. And my new friend could now sense my craving as he led me back into the mangroves. I could feel him eyeing my hungry hole from behind me. As we hiked across a grassy field towards a clump of bushes, my cock automatically got hard again. I spotted another Aborigine man with a huge cage on a bicycle, and I instinctively ducked behind a bush.

"It's okay," my friend told me. "Just a local fella catching mud crabs." I took his word for it.

After kissing passionately in the tangled forest, he finally lost his shirt and I watched his smooth black indigenous skin—skin that had been here since before time began—glistening in the sharp shards of the sun. I tried not to stereotype him as one of the naked "natives" I had masturbated to in *National Geographic*, but the erotic fantasy kept entering my head. Nude among the thick bushes and trees, keeping a lookout for sharp-toothed crocs, it was like having sex in a wild, prehistoric realm before clothes and cars and even bicycles. When depositing sperm was a thoughtless and almost automatic act, like breathing.

He pushed his thin, long dick inside of me, standing behind me. I could feel the tip of his uncovered dick touch the cum that was already in there. I thought I heard him chuckle at the feeling, like he knew I was already wet with the best lubricant on Earth—another man's semen. He pushed faster and faster into me, until I could feel the last man's sperm dislodge and coat the entire length of this new cock. It was sticky, like candy. I knew he wouldn't be able to last long with that silky feeling. He would need to breed me hard.

I knew what to do. I bent over and pushed all the way back on to him so he could feel it all. He smiled widely at me and laughed heartily on cue as he ejaculated what felt like a liter of sperm into my anal canal. The hot liquid shot and merged with the other stranger's load, creating a thick pudding that leaked onto the opening of my worn hole when he withdrew. It felt glorious, like life itself.

I didn't bother to come. My job was done. I stayed completely nude on our walk back to the parking lot, enjoying the feeling of two men's sperm leaking onto my butthole. The air felt all sticky and sweaty as well.

"You're from the U.S.?" my friend ventured.

"Yes. You're from Darwin?"

"I'm actually from Western Australia. So even though I'm a black fella, I don't understand the Aborigines here. They speak a totally different language."

"If you don't mind me asking, what is your skin?" I knew Aborigines were organized into animal clans they called *skins*, and now that a part of him was swimming deep inside me, I thought I could venture to ask such an intimate question.

"You're going to laugh." He flashed his toothy, crooked grin. "It's crocodile."

Savior for Sale in Ghana

The dance rehearsal took place in a kind of outdoor corral, made of four walls of wooden planks. Each space between the boards was filled with blinking eyes of children peering in from outside. The ancient African sky arched high above, and the moon rose above it all, gracefully outlining the reaching branches of a lone tree towering into the night.

The young performers came out in a line, each doing the "chicken dance" by flapping their bent arms like wings, a signature move of the Ewe tribe. They then moved into complex foot placements and dove their arms to the ground and back up. A row of drummers stood on the sidelines. The larger "talking drums" created the base beat while medium-sized and smaller drums built an alternating rhythm on top on them, fluctuating the sounds so that after some time my ears became aware of the intricacies of all the drumming and it began to sound like one hypnotizing, alternating orchestra. The moon cast a white gauze on it all, little faces stared between the boards, and the dancers' fluid and jerky movements all put me in a languid trance.

One male dancer with dreadlocks dangling out from under a brightly knitted cap looked directly at me. I looked back. He wore long spandex leggings that hugged his lanky, sinewy frame. This young man was the best dancer of them all, his floppy limbs perfectly controlled and timed to the music. He kept glancing at me. I wasn't hard to miss, being the only random white guy in the vicinity for miles. But his stares were far more concentrated than they should have been.

At the end of the rehearsal, he walked right up to me, shook my hand, smiled, and said, "My name is Savior." I made him repeat his name to make sure I had heard right.

"I'm Sebastian," and we snapped two of our fingers together at the end of our handshake, Ghanaian style.

"What are you doing tomorrow night?" Savior bluntly asked.

"Uh, I'm not sure yet."

"You will come to my house, I will give you drumming lessons." It wasn't an invitation, it was an order.

"Okay, that'd be fun."

He smiled again, the sweat trickling down from his cap. I hadn't had any African act so straightforward with me before.

The following night I was at the corral again, watching the same magnetic movements, watching Savior in his tight leggings. A warm dry breeze made its way down from the Sahel, miles and miles to the north of the endless Sahara. The rehearsal was shorter this time, and again Savior came up directly to me the minute it ended.

"Hello, Sebastian. You will come with me now."

Savior led me through the dark alleys of his little stucco village on the outskirts of the city of Accra. We passed open flames where old women sold tomatoes and chewing sticks, past kids shouting to each other, back into a courtyard with washing hung up everywhere, through a curtained door into a smaller room where Savior turned on a green overhead light. The soft alien illumination revealed posters glued up on the mud walls. One was of the Backstreet Boys. There were a few personal photographs too. A low bed took up most of the cement-floored space. It was a teenage boy's bedroom.

There were no chairs, so I sat on the bed. "How old are you, Savior?"

"I am twenty. You wait here, ok? I have to go to the shower quickly." I had seen the shared village toilets and showers before—I wouldn't want to feel my way through them in the dark.

I wandered around the room looking at photos of Ewe villagers and a couple of European men. Savior returned.

"Ok. We go to meet my friend."

I knew better than to question anything now. I followed him back through the alleys and over a dirt hill and down again and into a "garden," what Ghanaians call an open-air café. It was surrounded by walls and it had a juke box. We sat down at a small table and Savior plopped down very close to me. We ordered a couple of Fantas. It was understood that I would pay, but I didn't mind.

Savior looked deep into my eyes and told me, "I think you are a very beautiful man."

"Thank you, that's nice." I felt a warm gush. It doesn't take much to butter me up.

Savior quickly went through the "do you have a girlfriend, do you like girls?" routine and it became apparent where we were heading.

"Are you a gay?" he asked me point blank.

I was taken aback by the term—it seemed so progressive for the rustic setting.

"Yes, I am."

"I am a gay too." He took my hand in his and said, "I want to be your special friend, okay?"

"Okay." I smiled. It was nice to find family even in this deep neck of the woods.

Another young man walked up to us and I swiftly let go of Savior's hand. It was Savior's friend, Alex. He was around Savior's age and had a very handsome face, a lovely white smile and a disarming shyness about him. A sheepishness almost. He kept looking down at the ground and smiling as he spoke. He stood in stark contrast to Savior's bull-in-a-china-shop style of doing things. I suddenly, involuntarily, wished I were Alex's special friend instead of Savior's.

We all chitchatted and Savior explained to me that Alex had a special friend too—an older man from England who came to Ghana every few months to see him. It was pretty clear he helped finance Alex's life, and it was also getting pretty clear to me that's what Savior had in mind with his prior special friend request. Who could blame him? The price of a cup of coffee in the U.S. would buy a day's food for a whole family here. How often did a friendly thirty-something homo American walk through their Ewe village? Savior was smart to work every angle. In his head, there must have been some jealous competition with Alex for older white guys. I guess I was being paraded: *See, I can get a special friend to finance me too! And mine is more handsome!*

I began asking them questions about gay life in Ghana, and Savior and Alex told me there was not one, but two beaches where gays cruised each other, one near Accra and one near Cape Coast. There were a few nightclubs in Accra where gay guys could be found, although they were far from exclusively gay. They told me it was somewhat common for European men to have Ghanaian boyfriends.

On the walk back to Savior's place, he asked me, "Are you a king or a queen?"

"A king or a queen? What does that mean?"

"When you are in bed, are you a king or a queen?"

"Oh, I am usually a king."

He stopped walking and looked at me and smiled. "I am a king too!"

"Oh well, King. I'm sure we can work out something."

"But we are two kings."

"It doesn't matter. I'm sure we can be creative." I don't think he understood what I was saying.

We went back to Savior's bedroom and sat on the bed. After weeks of traveling alone, I was hungry for the feel of another body. I sat close to him and placed my face near his neck and breathed on him. He kept chattering away, getting up to pull things off a shelf and then hinting that I could purchase them. A carved hand, a miniature mask. They were cheap and exotic, so I gave him a few cedi, figuring he could use the money. But he wasn't selling what I really wanted. I think he didn't want any idea of sex to appear like it was too easy. It would instead be something I'd need to finance over the long term. But didn't he know a customer needs to be drawn in before they are hit with the hard sell? Sweet nothings in an ear or some form of romantic flirting would have helped his sales pitch.

If he was up for sale, then any good salesperson (or drug dealer) knows that a sample or two can create a dedicated consumer. I traced my finger down his leg and to the lanky bulge in his pants. I could see he was aroused. He finally asked me, "Are you big?"

"Let me show you." I unzipped my shorts and pulled my dick out so he could inspect it.

His face lit up. "It is nice." He began to fondle the pinkish flesh. He seemed to be sold.

I reached for his fly and he recoiled. I kept reaching anyway. After my long drought, I wasn't going to give up that easily. He finally pulled his cock out and it wasn't at all the black garden hose of racial clichés. I'm far from being a size queen, but the meager thing was surprisingly paltry. But no matter—we began to stroke each other, but Savior wouldn't stop jabbering on for some reason about this and that, like a leaky faucet that couldn't be stopped. What about, I can't remember, I just know it wasn't about sex. Was he really that nervous, or was he that inept as a salesperson?

We suddenly heard a noise outside the door. Savior stuffed himself back into his pants and got up to look. He said something to a cousin or neighbor or friend in Ewe, and I could hear feet shuffling away from the door. Savior then grabbed something else in the room to try to sell me as I reached for his crotch again. We resumed our positions with our hands down each other's pants.

"I want to be your special friend, Sebastian. I may come to America, to New Jersey later this year. I am invited to teach the drumming there. I can see you there."

"Okay, we'll see." My eyes were on his jet-black member with its distinct discolored scar below the head. A vision flashed in my mind of when I passed a little circumcision stand in another village with a sign that casually stated, "Get your child circumcised right here."

It wasn't a few minutes before we heard shuffling again. This time a boy came right through the door and nearly entered the room. I jerked my body up into a sitting position so my shirt would cover the hard-on poking out of my unzipped fly. Savior sternly told the person to go away, and I shoved my cock back into my underwear. I got up to leave. There was no such thing as privacy in Africa, and I thought I had better leave before the neighbors caught wind of the foreign pervert in their midst and chased him right out of the village.

Savior seemed sad that I had to exit so abruptly, even though it was pretty evident there would be no more sex than this innocent I'll-touch-yours-you-touch-mine. He wrote down his telephone number, and he explained how different people in the village would pick up the communal phone and then go and find him when I called. He really wanted me to call, and for me to see him in New Jersey. I told him I would.

He stopped me on my rush out the door and planted a simple, dry kiss directly on my lips. "This is the kiss of love without end."

For a microsecond, the magic and endlessness of Africa dwelled there on my lips, like an ancient potion.

"Ok," was all I could think to say.

I was supposed to leave Ghana the next day, but after waiting six hours at the muggy airport, my Ghana Airways flight back to New York was cancelled. Not for an hour or two, but for later in the week. All the passengers were put up in a hotel for two days for free.

I used the time to read in bed and to meander on a nearby public beach. I tried to find the rocky area where Savior and Alex had told me men cruise. I let the moist wind from the Gulf of Guinea flap my shirt open as I strode down the sand.

I saw an older, skinny man standing by some rocks not far away, looking at me. I sat down and waited to see what would happen. He promptly pulled his dick out of his pants. I was surprised he was so blatant. I went up to him and pulled my cock out of my Speedo, and he immediately began stroking it. He did it like it was an automatic habit, like a machine. When I grabbed his, he rubbed his thumb and forefinger together in the international sign to "pay up, sucker."

I had been giving *dashes* (the local word for tips) to everyone throughout my stay in Ghana for nearly every little thing. It's simply how the place works. It's not as bad as it sounds: The country's largest bill is 5,000 cedi—less than one U.S. dollar. Which is a lot in Ghana. That one bill can get you to the front of lines, get things delivered to your door, get you through any minor red tape. And from the looks of it, it can also get you random cock.

I handed the man a 5,000 cedi bill and he looked at it and seemed content. He kept playing with my cock as we stood in a private little nook amongst the rocks. I motioned for him to put my dick in his mouth, and he motioned back something that read "more money, fucker." I gave him another 5,000 cedi, and he sucked on me for a few uneventful mouthfuls, but it was clear he lacked the proficiency or the obligatory enthusiasm. You'd think he would have at least practiced once or twice on a friend before charging for it. He stood up again, and I played with his asshole. I handed him another 5,000 cedi as a hint. He didn't seem interested in that idea in the least. If his cocksucking skills were any indication, his anal talents must have been nil.

He finally blurted out, "You're money is no good, not enough." I didn't have any more bills on me, so I just quickly jerked my cock and shot my wad right in front of him, a volley of cum leaping across the wind and splattering on the rocks. Instead of being erotic, he must have interpreted it as a "take that then, bastard" gesture. He pulled up his loose trousers and stormed off up the rocks. I felt a little bad, like I had somehow cheated him at his own game. But even for less than two U.S. dollars, I've had ten times better blow jobs.

I walked back down the beach and I spotted an older Euro gent lounging on a chair. He was gray-haired and had on shorts. Next to him was a hot young Ghanaian boy in a snazzy bright tangerine Speedo. The locals normally never wear Speedos, so it was obvious the man had financed the boy's swimwear. The boy seemed too attentive to the man, the man seemed too appreciative of the attention, and the whole thing felt like a piece of theater. But everyone was getting what they wanted, I guess. You pay a man to bring you pizza to your front door, why not pay a boy to wear a hot Speedo next to you on the beach?

But the European was at least in his sixties, and I was just thirty-one. Was I really like him? Wasn't I too young to be financing a boy or paying for bad sex? My short track record in Ghana proved I evidently wasn't very good at either.

I had always seen myself as the boy, so maybe that's why I never called Savior during those two days of waiting for the plane. Maybe it was his pushiness, maybe it was his sly withholding of sex, maybe it was his cold calculations. Maybe it was the whole inequality of life between continents, of automatically being born into rich or poor places. Maybe it was just my ego.

When I got back home, that familiar strangeness came back of feeling that the trip had never happened at all. It was like waking up from a half-remembered dream. Ghana didn't really exist in this time. It was just a movie that one turned on and turned off and it was only alive when you were watching it.

I didn't call Savior, ever. I felt a bit guilty about it, even months afterwards, since I had said I would and all. I'm sure every time that communal village phone rang, he wanted it to be me on the line calling from America and professing my undying love and promising to give him anything he asked for. Maybe I should have sent him a few bucks. God knows he could have used it, and I did technically play with his dick. But there was little room for anything close to real emotion in Savior's ham-fisted attempts at a sexual business transaction. What if I had met him in New Jersey? What if we had actually started dating? What if I saw him lose his innocence? What if he somehow rejected me in the end for the great gleaming plastic-coated dream that is America?

I think I chose to keep Savior in my mind the way I left him, cozy in the vacuum of that little bubble of a village with the drums beating and the dancers flapping under the gauzy moonlight. Maybe the kiss of love without end was real in some other dimension. Maybe it should all be left there. I didn't want my life and the movie of Ghana to intermix. They were better apart, as disconnected entities. There was something pure in Ghana, something strong and true and unhindered and unhinged that would self-destruct once it reached the shores of America. Lands are kept far apart from each other for a reason, divided by oceans and languages, by deserts and peoples and epochs. It preserves their spirit in space. Let them stay that way.

A Tale of Two South Dakota Gay B&Bs

H ello?" My voice echoed bluntly through the downstairs of an obscure house in the Black Hills of South Dakota. Dirty dishes were piled everywhere, dirty laundry thrown helter skelter, dirty books teetering in crooked stacks, flies buzzing above the entire putrefaction.

I looked at my travel companion, Len. He liked to camp and wear shirts with holes in them, but even this was too much for him. It was the only gay bed and breakfast I had found for miles, for whole states around us. It had been a quest to get to the place, and we had no choice but to stay. It was late, we were on a remote dirt road surrounded by neatly-spaced pine trees. We needed shelter.

South Dakota is empty. It's rumored to have one gay bar, but we never found it. Barely more than 800,000 humans were alive in the entire state. And the land knew it was king here—it made sure you saw it stretch all the way to the horizon, past the horizon and onwards and upwards into the sky and the stars, in a show of arrogant dominance. Humans didn't matter here, they never would. You might as well give up. There were ten people per square mile in South Dakota, while New Jersey had 1,200 per square mile. How did gay guys find enough of themselves to even sparsely populate a bar here? And there were no gay bars in North Dakota, or in Wyoming next door. If we were going to have any kind of homo experience in the entire region, this B&B was, one way or another, going to be it.

Len and I had already slept in national park cabins, watched the strikes of lighting appear as the mythical thunderbirds over the badlands, driven through the bizarre rock spires of the Needles Highway, seen humanlike heads and figures carved into mountain faces, been surrounded by herds of roaming bison, eaten barbeque at a former firehouse in the Wild West downtown of Rapid City, and lost ourselves in the endless rolling landscape of the Sioux Nation, stopping at Wounded Knee massacre site in an attempt to understand the violence that is and was America.

We had done everything we were supposed to do. And now we found ourselves here. We were lone cowboys without a Brokeback Mountain. And it was getting dark.

We moved our bags into the disheveled living room, which was punctuated with ugly eagle motifs, cheap Indian rugs, and random pieces of arbitrary furniture. The shag carpet must have been harboring undisclosed dead things within its folds. It seemed to crack under our feet. We didn't take off our shoes. We tried to breathe through our mouths.

Eventually, after what seemed like days, weeks of us standing in the middle of a strange living room, daring each other to sit down, a couple of jolly older gents arrived in a pick-up truck. A plume of dust followed behind it, landing in the branches of the pines.

"Hey there! You guys ready to check in?" They plunked down on a splintered porch by a rancid hot tub that looked like a human-sized Petri dish. They busted open cans of beer from a cracked cooler, and smiled at the new flesh that fate had delivered right to their front door. "You guys can go nude in the Jacuzzi if you want." They both winked.

Apparently, the B&B was a rainbow-colored Venus flytrap that lured wayward gay travelers who had strayed too far from the safety of the tourist refuges of Mount Rushmore and The Badlands National Park. It was a homosexual Bates Motel.

Older gents, rustic cabins in the hills, not picking up after yourself—normally it would be, *sign me up!* But this B&B was more of a health hazard than a 'relaxed environment.' Len and I slept on crotchet blankets in a wood paneled room. We were too scared to actually get under the covers, to discover what was there. I found a stack of faded '70s porn magazines in the bathroom and thumbed through the stained photos of men with mustaches. I carefully placed them back like specimens.

After politely refusing breakfast in the morning, we escaped and I drove Len to the tiny Rapid City Airport. I think he was actually thankful he had to fly back home. But my journey would continue westward. I was driving alone, all the way to Yellowstone, up over mountains and past ancient medicine wheels made of little rocks in fields and past oppressive skies pushing down on the top of my car and the edges of infinity that were jagged and smooth at the same time. I had to make sure I had enough gasoline and Coca Cola and peanuts and patience, always patience to scan the few radio stations over and over again, trying to find something, anything, to fill up the void of the car.

The only other gay B&B my careful research had presented me was just off the interstate near the Wyoming border. I called up and booked a room.

"My partner and I will be happy to have you stay here," replied the voice on the other end. It sounded hygienic enough.

The next day I drove through rolling plains so beaten down by wind that the grass blades permanently leaned to one side, in surrender. It was the natural habitat of 18-wheeler trucks barreling through, like sailboats driven by gale force winds.

I steered my car off the safety of the east-west freeway and ventured exactly northward, where the map warned me there would be nothing. I would be okay, I wouldn't be going far.

I coasted up and over the gigantic frozen waves of hills, with their furry coats of grass. I finally found a large, lonely trailer perched upon the top of a gusty hill and followed its long gravel driveway. It was old but looked clean, like it had been sandblasted by wind. The rickety wooden steps to the door had some metal objects and pots and things that looked like they were parts of things, not things in and of themselves. A small storage shed sat nearby, the kind you find at a gardening supply store, and I couldn't figure how it hadn't been blown over yet.

I knocked on the metal door long and hard, no answer. I sat down on the broken steps, next to a dirty ashtray. I gazed at the start of a heavy, arduous sunset over the never-ending ridge of America.

At last I heard steps, and after one final burst of knocking, the door swung open to reveal a slim man in white Hanes underwear with a mustache and huge bags under his eyes. "Are you Sebastian?"

"Yes."

"Come in." There was no place to sit inside the trailer. Every available surface was stacked with piles of clothes, books, dirty dishes, items, items, items, items, too many items for human eyes to individually itemize. It didn't really feel like a surprise. I evidently hadn't learned my lesson about dirty gay B&B Venus flytraps in South Dakota.

The underwear man blurted out: "I'm sorry I haven't had a chance to clean up. You see, my partner died yesterday."

I stood there. Then I simply put my hand on his shoulder. He cried and cried, telling me his partner of fourteen years had had a heart attack, that the ambulance had come yesterday, that it was right after I called, that I could still stay the night if I wanted to. He was lucid and disoriented at the same time. It looked like he had been asleep a long time before I arrived. He pushed aside a stack of magazines and we sat and shared a cigarette. And I genuinely felt sorry for the man, who seemed to be happy that someone, anyone, any human, any stranger the wind blew in, was now here with him in the trailer.

That night, he asked me to have sex with him, and we did in his and his partner's bed. He lay down on his stomach with his hairy buttocks separated for my cock to lie between. We used hand lotion, that's all he had. He stared straight ahead at a fuzzy porn tape and then closed his eyes and sighed heavily and fully, like he was taking a stiff drink of whiskey to suppress pain. I wanted to fuck him gently, tenderly, but he demanded to be pounded. I piled into him like I was digging a ditch, and he wanted the harshness of the reality of it to transport him outside of his body.

The haunting wind howled around the thin walls of trailer, a dollhouse standing in the face of all physical odds, alone on top of a hill that was a wide-open wind tunnel. The gusts threatened to blow the whole place down, but I kept driving my way inside him, further and further into him. He said he loved it, and he did. I came inside him, like an offering. It was all I could really give him.

Some would call it the ultimate mercy fuck in a dirty trailer on an empty hill in the middle of nowhere America. But I felt that for at least one night in my life I had given sanctuary to a stranger from the unpredictable elements of the ruthless and unremitting world outside.

Glass Walls in Hawaii

I had been in love, or lust, with Ben for many years. Actually, since I was twenty-eight, when I had first met him on the gay portion of Waikiki Beach, his white rippled torso gleaming in the stark sunshine, a dimpled chin and sandy brown hair and bulging Speedo and an aw-shucks Okalahoma smile. He was in his late thirties, and gorgeous, and he knew it. And I knew it, and the whole beach knew it.

His cartoon-chiseled form was made all the more appealing by a human who would peek out from under it every now and then. He was a little insecure, as if he didn't know how to deal with the gifts the universe had bestowed upon him, and the more he tried to hide this insecurity, the more obvious it was, which just made him sexier. He was such a man, and such a boy. More specifically: a sweet boy trapped in a grown man's body. Which was my specific fetish that, for some bizarre reason, aroused me to no end (and still does). Probably because I am a grown man trapped in a boy's body. Every pot has its lid.

Ben wore tight, thick, box-cut swimming trunks, and the white of his stomach skin showed all the ripples of his abdomen. He would turn over, and the two huge basketballs of his perfect bubble butt seemed to almost bounce through the material. Then he'd flip over again, and his bulge was proud and protruding up to the tropical sun, straight to the gods. I could trace the thin trail of belly button hair to the very top of his pubes, and I imagined how soft they would be, and match the color of his head, and how I would love to have rested my face there in the sunshine, the hairs of his scrotum tickling my nose as his balls shrank and grew and rolled around in the smooth sack in the tropical heat. Even his sweat would smell sweet. I couldn't imagine an inch of him not to be perfect—even the small brown moles on his back seemed to be expertly, artistically spaced apart.

Like most insecure people, he loved people to look at him, and hated it too, and loved it, and hated it, and loved it. He lay on the gay grassy lawns at the Queen's Surf Beach, and he appeared so creamy vanilla in contrast to the golden-brown sea of Japanese, Filipino, Polynesian, mixed-race, and overly-tanned Caucasian hides all around him. He stood out, and I could feel the eyes of passersby sail over to his body which was splayed out for their visual enjoyment. I understood—after having lived in the islands for years—a really white Mainland *haole* from Okalahoma now seemed foreign to me too.

Haole: "*ha*" means *breath*, "*ole*" means *without*. So basically, it's the Hawaiian word for a dead person. Makes sense: Hawaiians were only really white when they were corpses. And the term *haole* alluded to the fact that white people could sometimes be a little dead inside as well.

Queen's Surf lies at the easternmost section of Waikiki Beach. It's near the grand, abandoned Natatorium, just past where Kapahulu Avenue meets Kalakaua Avenue. The 1920s Natatorium, a saltwater swimming pool built in glorious Hawaiian Beaux-Arts architecture, is where local Olympic gold medal holder Duke Kahanamoku took his swims in tight trunks, his heroic rippled muscled bronzed body on display to all the eyes in the outdoor stadium. In the "Homolulu's" gay heyday of 1970s, there was a bar within walking distance of Queen's Surf Beach. It was called The Blow Hole. Guys would come in with sand in their swimsuits, strip down at the bar, and jump into the Blow Hole's large heated pool, which would be jam-packed with jostling flesh by evening's end, like a tank of live eels. But then AIDS hit and then the local Mormons and the Catholics joined forces and then the Internet arose and gay travelers discovered other more exotic places to be gay and the height of Honolulu's gay glory days became a forgotten memory and now families can be found right along Queen's Surf. In true Waikiki fashion, a grocery store now sits where the Blow Hole blew its way into history.

Behind Queen's Surf Beach are the huge, lush grounds of Kapiolani Park. Under the watchful eye of the extinct volcanic crater of Diamond Head, men would sneak back into the park's tennis courts, bathrooms, and bushes as night fell. I knew better than to venture there—on statewide TV, I had witnessed the police drag handcuffed men out of the park, their faces shown to families and co-workers and the entire population of The Aloha State. On an island this small, in an island group this tiny and remote, there was no anonymity, no escape from who you really were.

That's why I usually went after tourists like Ben. They'd soon be on a plane, never to return—at least not 'til next season. I was safe fooling around in the big city of Honolulu, two or three islands over from where my boyfriend and lived, depending on how you counted.

Ben seemed to like my clumsy flirtations, but kept his distance. He glanced around out of the corners of his eyes, darting back and forth at his potential predators, then back to me. Darting forward to the sandy "puppy pit" where the twinks hung out in front of Queen's Surf, then back to the "bone yard" on the beach's back lawns where all the old queens played bridge in bikinis on folding chairs. I couldn't tell what he wanted. I kept thinking he wanted me to leave, then he'd sit and laugh at my jokes. He pushed, he pulled, it worked. I was smitten. And I was insecure enough just to be glad this adonis paid me any attention at all.

That night, Ben held my hand under a table at a gay bar. He asked about my boyfriend, but didn't let go of my hand. He seemed to comment derogatorily about me being a massage therapist, even though I was licensed had gone to school for two years and my profession had nothing (or not much) to do with sex. I tried to give him the answers that would make him happy. I tried to make him happy. That his gorgeous face and body and hand even spent so much time with me was all my ego needed.

We didn't have sex, but I was satiated nonetheless.

A couple years later, I called Ben up when I was in his hometown of San Diego. "Sorry, I'm just crazy busy with work," he told me. "Call me next time when you're in town." My heart sank. I drove the freeway back to L.A., slouched down low in my seat, trying not to be devastated by a complete stranger.

My Achilles Heel is my tenacity in the face of aloofness. The following year, I was in San Diego again and I called him. "Uh, sure, why don't you meet me and my boyfriend for a drink."

Boyfriend? My heart sank again, but I still needed a Ben fix, just to see him, just to be near him, just to have him pay some attention to me, even in front of his stupid boyfriend.

His boyfriend was an older guy, nice enough, bland enough, not dashing enough. I wondered why Ben was with him. Was it money? I couldn't tell. Of course, I was jealous just sitting in their presence, and I slowly got the feeling that I didn't have enough money to keep Ben interested in me. Even a fuck was out of the question now that he had got himself hitched, the bastard. I also got the feeling that the only reason Ben was interested in seeing me was because now I lived in New York City and worked for some big, impressive magazines, and I wasn't some twinky "massage therapist" trying to pick up a hunky tourist who was out of his league.

I should have given up on Gorgeous Ben, but I haven't. When I met him a year later in San Diego, he was finally single. We went out for drinks, he showed me his Craftsman home in a nice neighborhood, and somehow I finally got his white torso over me naked in bed and a condom over my erection aimed at his perfect pink hole. I couldn't believe I would at last be deep inside my fantasy, and it was just as good, terrifyingly good, as I had imagined it would be. I was so nervous fucking his perfect white globes of flesh, I was nearly shaking. I made sure to penetrate him the way he wanted. I came inside the condom only when I knew he had already spurted his load all over my hairy chest. He giggled a little afterward, almost embarrassed. I couldn't believe he let me spend the night with him in his home, in his bed, with his roommate in the other bedroom. I didn't cuddle up with him too hard, although I wanted to smother him, I wanted him to smother me with his hard white flesh, I wanted to kiss him so hard his tongue would be sucked right out of his mouth. But I made sure not to be too desperate. The years of my pursuit had finally led me inside of him—I had to be careful not to get shut out again too soon.

That morning, after his shower, I placed my knees on his hard wood floors and he bent over slightly and let me suck on his perfect pink asshole, so clean and smooth and right. I pulled his globes apart as far as I could, but they were still so deep that their weight and volume nearly suffocated me. I took great gulps of air, holding my breath, diving deep into the pink abyss until I couldn't breathe anymore. If I died here like this, what a way to go! I shot a huge spatter of semen across the floor in appreciation, and then quickly cleaned it up with toilet paper and flushed it away. He giggled again.

A month later, I invited him out to Palm Springs for the weekend. I would pay for the whole thing. He accepted, which confirmed my suspicions he may be a gold digger. Who cared? I liked the idea of a younger guy objectifying and paying for an older guy—there was something upside-down about it that made it kinky. Ben laid out his white torso in a Speedo by the pool at our upscale gay guesthouse. No nude sunbathing was allowed—I had made sure not to take him to a sleazy resort where anyone could have their way with him, or vice versa. I was still a little too nervous about losing my prized possession once again. I tried not to be jealous about the guys ogling him, but instead tried to think of him as my trophy boy, like I was the brains and the money and he was the muscle. That scenario turned me on.

There was a hot, oily, brown Latin by the pool. When we went upstairs, Ben left the door open, and posed to the Latin below. He smiled. Ben mentioned wanting to have a three-way with him. I tried to not be jealous again. It sounded hot in theory, but I knew my insecurity was way too flimsy for that. I laughed off his request like it was a joke or something, and shut the door. And locked it.

When Ben would look at you, he looked past you out to some far distance. He was like one of those thin clouds high up in the stratosphere. Being with him was like talking to someone behind a pane of clear glass—you could see him and hear him, but there was something opaque between you, something that you could not touch, and the glass couldn't be broken. You were always left staring at the beautiful contents, unsure of what you were looking at exactly.

But on the way home from Palm Springs, that glass between us shattered.

"Don't drive that way!" Ben ordered, reaching over to honk the horn. "Why do you call your niece *baby*? You should call her *princess*!" he scolded. And a hundred other unattractive comments and traits that finally burst to the surface in a great rush, like bragging over his cell phone to his friends that he had had an all-expenses paid weekend in Palm Springs. Suddenly, I looked over to him, and his chiseled face and cleft chin appeared disjointed, Cubist. He literally became tainted right before my eyes, as his carefully formed persona of all those years melted and formed a puddle, and if you looked closely, you could see streaks of mildew that had been hidden in the folds of the creamy whiteness. The whole container and its contents had gone off, and the rancid insides suddenly were spilling out.

I kept my mouth shut the whole ride back. I couldn't wait to get him out of my car. My heart broke once again, but this time it was not for unrequited infatuation, but the fact that people could keep their masks so firmly in place for so long over so much distance and so much time. I had been staring at the surface of the glass so hard, I had never actually seen all the way through it.

Burning Man and the Temporary World

A completely nude and bearded man stood at a small booth and instructed me to stop my car. I rolled down the window. A gust of white dust filled my lungs, and the setting sun glittered off his sandy body. The wide desert sky shot blue up into the solar system. The naked man grinned and said to me, "Welcome to Burning Man."

"It's my first time here," I meekly muttered.

"A virgin!" the man announced at the top of his lungs, and a few others yelled back with catcalls.

"Get out of the car," he ordered.

Who was I to argue with a totally exposed man in the middle of the desert? I did I was told, already feeling like I hadn't undressed enough for the occasion. He led me to a large bell and told me to pick up the crowbar dangling from it. "Hit it!"

I smacked it hard, with a resounding *dong*, so to speak. People applauded.

"You're a virgin no more," he declared.

I carefully steered my car along a long sandy road, reading each of the small but intricate signs along its edge.

"We've all been raised on television …" the first one said.

"… to believe that one day we'd all be millionaires and movie gods and rock stars …" said the second.

"… but we won't. And we're slowly learning that fact …" read the third.

"… and we're very … very … pissed off!" the fourth proclaimed.

A fifth sign attributed these words to the author of *Fight Club*, Chuck Palahniuk, who I knew was gay, even though the signs didn't disclose that. I would quickly learn that labels like gay or straight or bi or whatever meant nothing out here in the desert of Burning Man, where each person stood as their own unique god, each a specific creation, and the individual with all his/her/its quirks and dreams reigned supreme here.

My car crawled along at five miles an hour as the speed limit dictated as I approached the entrance to Black Rock City. I was about 110 miles north of Reno, outside the miniscule village of Gerlach, a former company town for United States Gypsum Corporation with a current population of 500. How these few isolated desert dwellers coped with 50,000 people from all over the world flooding their bone-dry backyard was beyond me. The blank land here was transformed every year into a tangible electric fantasy, during the week before Labor Day, when Burning Man rises out of a dusty plain where the ancient Lake Lahontan once covered 8,500 square miles of Nevada. What's left is a flat mountain-ringed basin dusted with gypsum, a super fine mineral used for drywalls and for coagulating tofu. This white gypsum powder is as delicate as talcum and so thin you don't even notice you're inhaling it until you blow your nose and a mixture of white and brown comes out, like you're a drug addict.

Before me, Black Rock City appeared—a combination of African refuge camp, *Mad Max* movie set, and the Emerald City. The sheer size of what I was encountering was astounding: A sprawling campus of 50,000 people who had erected a post-apocalyptic desert metropolis of tents, domes, roads, and structures in a 1.5-mile diameter semicircle in the middle of nowhere. The encampment is said to become the third-largest city in the state when it's all put up. And it all began as an impromptu bonfire on Baker Beach in San Francisco on summer solstice in 1986, when a few friends spontaneously burned a 9-foot wooden form of a man. The participants said later it was a spontaneous act of "radical self-expression." Like any true revolution, the thing took on a life of its own, beyond human control.

The spectacular, organic, nonprofit party that is now Burning Man is allowed to occur on federal land owned by the U.S. Bureau of Land Management. The agency dictates that every speck of trash—every cigarette butt and every used tampon—must be picked up by the event's organizers, or else they face a heavy fine. But it's rarely paid. "The Playa" where this provisional city is built is always left in its exact unadulterated form right after the weeklong event. If you came back a few days after it's all torn down, you'd never even know Burning Man had occurred. How this feat is pulled off in the paranoid twenty-first century is a magical mystery no one can fathom—even the eight dystopian years of the George W. Bush era couldn't exterminate this hippy/techo celebration to end all hippy/techo celebrations.

It's the closest thing the modern world has to an annual mirage.

Trying to explain Burning Man to the uninitiated is like trying to describe color to a blind person. It was a realm of visions I'd never seen before. Along the dusty streets I passed an elderly topless woman with pink sunglasses and a sarong. A drag queen in green spandex and platform shoes casually followed her. Then a heterosexual man in a grandma-style mumu and a floppy white hat. They were all as nonchalant as if they were shopping at the local mini-mall.

I followed the curved arms of the city, each of its avenues in alphabetical order. Each festooned camp I passed stated its theme with a sign: "The Church of Chill," "Baby Seal Club," "Cirque Ber-zerk," "Emotional Baggage," and one of my favorites for some reason, "TBD." Each was a complete work of art in itself, some with scaffold-ing, walls, roofs, tents, murals, catwalks, couches, yards, and bars.

I found myself swerving around "art cars" and floats that came out of nowhere and skidded across the desert in front of me. It was like a living cartoon—vehicles in the shape of cats, ships, horses, spiders, jellyfish, boom boxes, and yes, cupcakes. On wheels. With people inside, driving them. Fully functional. You didn't need to be on drugs here: you automatically felt like you were.

I stopped and asked one dreadlocked girl if she knew of the camp I was searching for, called "Comfort & Joy." She looked at me. "Honey, there are over 50,000 people here. I haven't got a god-damn clue."

Somehow I came upon "Comfort & Joy." It's one of the main gay camps at Burning Man—another is called "Jiffy Lube," known for its dark room tented maze where gays and "curious men" sucked and jacked each other off. The gals who like gals congregated at a less sexual encampment, the bluntly named "Camp Cunt." "Com-fort & Joy" consisted of two circus tents and a row of inflatable fuchsia-colored palm trees with banners waving in the hot breeze. An outdoor shower bag with a hose was strung up between two poles, with no walls.

I parked my car and asked some of the semi-clad guys sitting at the makeshift outdoor kitchen if they knew where to find my friend Bradford. It was he who had told me all about "Comfort & Joy."

"Ask Kitten," was the universal reply.

I found Kitten, a tall, bleach-blond, skinny, twenty-something man in a sparkly blue miniskirt and matching eye shadow. He was evidently the chief of the camp. "Oh, I think Bradford was here yesterday. He's not staying here. I don't know where he is, sorry."

"Oh. Is it okay if I set up my tent here?" I tepidly inquired.

"Sure."

Was there such a thing as the word "no" at Burning Man?

Under a growing night, I erected the tent I had purchased at the Walmart in Reno, put on a pair of tight black swim trunks, filled a plastic bottle with tequila and juice, and ventured out into the depths of "The Playa." It's the empty center of the semicircle city, where the monolithic seven-story Burning Man sculpture stands with his arms out, overseeing all.

Like a foreign movie without subtitles, it's hard to explain everything that happened next. In the heat of the dark night, with forms and lights and sounds all around me, I saw apparitions. That were real. I passed by an actual flamethrower target range, with participants in fire retardant suits. I walked through an Old West town filled with cowboys with electric lights strung all over them. A metal hand three stories tall waved at me. I spoke with a gate-keeper at a dungeon who said I could come back to confess my sins to the judge, who would decide my punishment accordingly. I passed a "Psychiatric Help—5 Cents" booth where a lady with a leg cast told me I should simply do whatever work I enjoyed—fuck money. I dodged more cupcakes on wheels.

I expected Tina Turner as Auntie Entity in *Mad Max III* to make an appearance any minute. Just then, as if the universe had read my mind, I turned and saw a huge dome with the word "Thunderdome" on it in bright lights. I didn't think I had consumed that much tequila.

I climbed up the enormous jungle-gym-like structure and gazed down at two men in fantastic warrior wear hitting each other with what looked like giant Q-tips. The dangling crowd cheered above. "Two men enter, one man leaves!" A drag queen on stilts used her huge magical staff to knight the winner.

The rest of my night was a psychedelic swirl of riding on a musical pirate ship, huddling amid lingerie-clad girls at a bonfire, watching nude karaoke, playing neon miniature golf, and dancing on a raised outdoor platform terrace under a desert dawn with video screens flashing images at me.

Black Rock City had no advertisements, no sponsors, no money, nothing to buy and sell. Although it looked like Auntie Entity's Bartertown, it was actually its antithesis. Everyone brought in their own supplies, and no one had any sense of ownership. Everywhere I went, people freely gave to each other whatever was asked—booze, clothing, water, food, shelter, company, sex. I kept hearing the mantra "The Playa gives," and it was exactly correct. No one inquired about—and no one knew—each other's real names, jobs, incomes, backgrounds. It didn't matter. Everyone was on the same level desert ground. I never saw a fight, a drug overdose, rudeness, or cruelty. For the first time in my life, I witnessed 50,000 people living as one unit. Transcendental is an overused word, but that's precisely what this was.

When I finally staggered back to "Comfort & Joy" that first night, I found my tent had blown up in the wind and was sitting lopsided next to my car like a deflated balloon. That shelter idea obviously wasn't going to work in the Mars-like elements.

I peeked inside "Comfort & Joy's" dimly lit large main circus tent. Mattresses and cushions were strewn all about. Some guys were eating in one corner, some others smoking pot in another, some others snoring in another, and some others French kissing in another. Some had clothes on, some didn't. Some knew each other, others were quickly getting to know each other quite well. Men—gay, straight, or whatever—simply sojourned from the other parts of Black Rock City to see what the gay camp was all about.

I grabbed my sleeping bag and decided to try to make a go of it in this communal space. Between the snores, grunts, and guitar riffs, I hoped to get some sleep.

I awoke to a flapping tent edge next to my face. I rubbed my eyes, and the gypsum dust just dug into my skin further. It was still dark out.

I felt a finger—not mine—gently tugging at my underwear band. I looked down at a large male hand and then looked up to see the smiling face of a naked man lying next to me. He was tall, muscular, African-American. Without me saying anything, he tenderly pulled my underwear all the way off. My cock was already hard from my sleep, and it bounced up out of the jockey shorts like a jack in the box, like it was on a wire.

His hand grabbed it and began massaging. I didn't move. The man inched his smooth torso closer to me, and I could feel his skin heating mine. He moved his mouth over my dick, slowly coating it with saliva. It felt amazing.

His lanky, graceful body was soon over mine, and he was carefully lifting my legs on to his shoulders. He spat in his hand and rubbed it all over my asshole. Luckily, his cock wasn't a clichéd black Godzilla, since it was soon inside of me, pumping in an unhurried, deliberate rhythm, just how I like it.

He leaned down and whispered in my ear, "God. Feels so good."

I panted in agreement.

"I love doing this in front of everyone," he informed me. I glanced out of the corner of my eye, but couldn't tell if anyone in the crowded tent was even bothering to notice our grinding figures. But it made me excited to think that someone was.

After a long time of kissing me and rubbing his shaved head all over my chest, his breathing became heavy and I knew what was about to happen. He held his cock still inside of me, and I could feel every swell and pump of his orgasm deep in me. He held it there for a long time, emptying himself into me, every drop. I clenched down on his cock in return, milking it with my butt muscles. He eventually pulled himself out, smiled once again, and I fell back to sleep with his essence now a part of me.

I never saw him again. But I was pretty sure he hadn't been a mirage. I could still feel his cum up in me the next morning.

The next morning, the wind was beginning to whip up the dust, but it wasn't going to stop me from exploring the city. I tied a bandana across my face, covering my mouth and nose. I approached one of the guys at the camp and asked him if he knew where to get any coffee. "Sure, it's at center camp. I'll take you there."

Then he told me, "I'm just going to go naked, since there's a dust storm coming. You'll need these." He handed me a pair of ski goggles, which offered much more protection than my flimsy sunglasses. I took his goggle offering and shed all my clothes as well, following his example. We'd just get caked with fine dust in every nook and cranny anyway, clothes or not.

We walked nude like this, wearing just goggles and scarves with water bottles and tennis shoes. We walked down the shifting sand streets of the momentary metropolis, and the wind soon turned into a full-fledged sand storm, like in *Dune*. Thick white walls rose all around us. We were in a thin airy bowl of alabaster soup. Strange figures came out of the walls—people on decorated bicycles, men in robes carrying lanterns, fuzzy headlights of vehicles. There were no sounds, just the howling of wind and sand and all the elementary elements.

I knew we were getting lost, but wasn't that the point of Burning Man? After lurching for a half hour through the warm storm, our naked skin being blasted by it, I made out a sign that read "Flying Monkey Circus."

"Let's go in there," I yelled to my new naked friend, my voice muffled by the bandana. I couldn't see his eyes through his goggles, just the nod of his head. His hair was covered in white powder, like a founding father.

We ducked in through an entrance, and then the structure opened up with two stories of scaffolding swaying in the wind, but holding its own. A main courtyard had no roof. We lifted our goggles and gazed upon various *Star Wars*-like figures gyrating to 1920s music blaring over loudspeakers. We could make out costumes and states of male and female undress under the veneer of dust caking everyone. Two grown man naked in goggles? We fit right in.

We looked up, and a figure on a trapeze flew above us overhead. A bar counter was lined with random bottles of liquor, and someone told us to help ourselves. I filled up my water bottle with vodka, and was quickly drunk. Before I knew it, my new friend and I were taking turns flying completely nude on the trapeze, dust dancing about our heads while the song "Yes, We Have No Bananas" kept blaring. While swinging through the air, my friend accidentally kicked a dangling disco ball with his sneakers. It went flying out the entrance of the "Flying Monkey Circus" while the crowd roared and clapped.

My new friend was Troy, a "Burner" in his late forties. He was very thin, slightly hairy, Caucasian, with a shaved head and a goatee. He lived in San Francisco, and this was his fourth Burning Man. He always stayed at "Comfort & Joy." I didn't ask too much more, and he didn't offer. It didn't matter—the setting was the star of the show at Burning Man, and its characters were meant to be the window dressing, not the main course.

Troy took me under his wing for the next few days, and I would fuck him on all fours in his tent when the wind died down, and then we'd go and discover strange corners of the city at night, chatting with random humans along the way. If the weather was hot, we'd be naked. If it wasn't, I'd wrap my sleeping bag around myself and he would wear a huge fur coat he had borrowed from a friend. He pointed out the communal bicycles that anyone could take once another rider had parked them. He told me about the huge art installations set up so deep back in The Playa that most people never saw them. He told me about how I needed to put vinegar on my feet to counteract the cracks that form on your heels from the gypsum. I, in turn, became his Burning Man protégé, his virgin who needed guidance. We became brothers in arms, looking after each other as desert companions, comrades through the vodka and the windstorms. We didn't really snuggle or kiss—I guess we were more like stranger fuck buddies. But it was nice to have someone handy to comment on everything with, so you didn't feel like you were the only one having a hallucination. The sheer intensity of the Burning Man experience was one you couldn't keep to yourself. It was akin to the last book of the Bible, where the long hard battle is over and everyone is beaming and glowing and walking on streets of gold and the joy is beyond worlds, and beyond the Earthy realm.

Kitten later said to me, "Thanks for spending so much time with Troy. He's a good friend of mine and he said he was having a hard time connecting with anyone this Burning Man. He really enjoys hanging out with you."

On the last Saturday night, Troy and I watched the Burning Man burn with gigantic pyrotechnic explosions worthy of a Jerry Bruckheimer movie. Thousands screamed and cheered as the megastructure flamed and fell over the course of an hour or so. A group of people danced around his embers and his dying fires all night long, and I sat and gazed at their shadows. There's a reason why humans are tribal and need rituals—it's justified and it's ancient. There must be wild left in the world, or we are doomed.

The next evening, I climbed to the top of the temple, the multi-story intricate wooden structure that was a mash-up of Thai, Western, and Surrealist architecture. Anywhere else, it would have been a permanent landmark. Here, it served as a public shrine to departed loved ones. The temple was covered with personal scrawls, poems, photos, drawings, and heartbreaking dedications to the dead and the gone. Everyone gets it—it's rare to find a human being who has spent some time on Earth without having lost someone. Small groups of people stood on the temple's platforms and hugged each other and cried softly. The lights of Black Rock City sparkled below like moonlight on an empty ocean.

I found a black marker and wrote "Hi Mom" on one of the pillars. She would have liked Burning Man.

On Sunday night, a smaller crowd—but still in the thousands—watched as the temple was set on fire. The throng was silent and still. I glanced at faces, all streaked with tears. The temple methodically burned and crashed down, down, down to the ground, one huge crimson log after the next until it was no more. It was the great release—the soul of the fleeting city, transformed, transitioned, carried away by the wind and the night.

Jack Kerouac wrote: "Accept loss forever." Expert spiritual advice from the departed.

The whole week I was at Burning Man, I never found my friend Bradford, who had coaxed me into coming here in the first place.

Troy and I didn't keep in touch after Burning Man. But a whole year later, I found myself back at "Comfort & Joy" once again: the same circus tents, the same fuchsia palm trees, the same tangle of bodies on cushions. The temple, the man and the camps all looked slightly different, yet familiar, like a recurring dream.

I spotted Troy, once again in his a birthday suit and wearing goggles, just like I left him. I ran up to him.

"Hey, how are you?" I greeted.

He looked at me blankly. He had no idea who I was. I stood there like an idiot. "You don't remember me, do you?"

He smiled and said no. I smiled back, and then just walked away.

I guess some incidents in life are temporary by their very nature, meant to be deconstructed and set on fire, burned down and thrown into the spinning dust of the desert wind. And loss is forever and must always be accepted.

A Sore Orifice in Mykonos

A group of men stood on the stone terrace, overlooking the mythical Greek sunset over the Aegean Sea. Holy beams of streaking sunlight shot down through the layer of clouds as the maroon sun ducked down underneath them. The men were German, Swedish, British, and/or Dutch—let's just say *Euro*—and wearing an array of tight bikini swimwear, one or two of them completely naked. They smoked cigarettes and sipped ouzo and snapped photos and when the sun made its final victorious bolt below the horizon, the crowd cheered.

Such was another day at the Elysium Hotel, one of just two gay clothing-optional resorts in all of Greece. Both properties happened to make their home on the isle of Mykonos. The crowd of men was all facing in the direction of Mykonos' neighboring isle of Delos. This was appropriate. I had already taken a ferry to sacred, uninhabited Delos, the birthplace of the sun god Apollo and the moon goddess Artemis. I had taken photos of the two perfectly symmetrical and enormous oval testicles mounted on top of a pillar there from 300 BC. The shaft of the pillared penis abruptly ended just above its magnificent scrotum. The monumental cock had evidently been stolen by some phallus-worshipper from days gone by.

The phallus was the symbol, the embodiment, of Dionysus, the god of wine and of the life-force, the god of epiphany, "the god that comes." Disney cartoons portrayed Dionysus as a fat and happily alcoholic, but the ancient Greeks depicted him as a mysterious naked androgynous boy holding a wine goblet, who drew you in with his sweet and almost innocent intoxication. The isle of Delos was home to a whole sanctuary built for Dionysus, and the Delos itself was in the dead center of the circular chain of the 220 Cyclades Islands.

It was a bull's eye spiritual vortex, an opening, an orifice that lasted for over 4,000 years like a black hole in the center of a galaxy, emitting light and energy and sucking all of its secrets inside of itself.

I discovered that Dionysus is still quite alive and well in Mykonos. He hovered over my entire stay on the island, however circuitously. Alcohol, wine, penises, and sexual life-force—Mykonos was reeking of all of the above like a gravitational pull of dark and light.

The Elysium Hotel was owned by Vassilis, the sixty-something salt-and-pepper Greek. He tried to explain it all to me: "There's something metaphysical about Mykonos, some vibe. I don't know why. Ask God!"

Vassilis opened Greece's first-ever gay hotel in 1990. The Elysium is a lovely blue and white affair (in the traditional Greek colors) with a small gym and a restaurant and a clothing-optional pool, all perched up on a dry hillside with ocean panoramas. The year 1990 may sound a little late to get into the gay hotel game, but this is Greece. The land that invented man-boy love and "Greek active" and "Greek passive" and the idealized male nude (heck, the Greeks, particularly Sappho, even invented Lesbianism on the isle of Lesbos) somehow morphed into one of the most closeted modern societies in all of Europe, dominated by the towering ubiquitous domes of the Greek Orthodox Church. Athens didn't even have a gay pride parade until 2005.

Then how did Mykonos become renowned as a balls-to-the-wall, tits-out party island? Why was it synonymous with sex and sand and naked hot Euro-dudes?

"I think it's the island's history of being a multicultural center of trade and commerce," Vassilis tried to fathom. "The Mykonos people were always very open-minded and tolerant."

Ever since I was a kid, I had heard legends of Mykonos' Super Paradise Beach, where homosexual men frolicked all day in the nude, like erect prancing satyrs (sans nymphs) in the stark Aegean sunlight. I knew I was supposed to be there with them. As a prepubescent boy, I would take off all my clothes and walk around the forest nude, wishing I had a beach full of naked men at my disposal. When I finally set eyes on the well-trampled bit of sand that is "Super Paradise," lined with neat rows of wooden chaise lounges and umbrellas backed by an open-air bar blasting canned pop music, I realized my fantasies were a much better destination than this reality.

It was back in the innocent, coke-fueled 1970s when gay jetsetters followed in the footsteps of their idols Elizabeth Taylor and Jackie O. and the celebs who put Mykonos on the globe's fun-time party map. God knows what went down on Super Paradise back then, but by the end of the twentieth century, cheap flights were shuttling the riff-raff Euro hoards to Mykonos. Straights trying to be hip long ago edged out the sunbaked gay satyrs from Super Paradise. I scanned its sands, and spotted oiled-up topless babes with fake boobs alongside their greasy boyfriends, who were happy to have everyone look at their hot chicks' racks.

The homos knew when a gig was up, and the ever vigilant gay gnomes found new cruising grounds a couple of coves over at Elia Beach. The structure of Elia was perfect for the gays anyway. It too had wooden chaise lounges and umbrellas and an outdoor bar, but there was a nearby convenient bluff carved with rocky outcroppings, tailor-made for how-do-you-do interludes under the white-washed Greek sun. The satyrs persevered here and thrived.

And it was at Elia Beach, among the jutting cliffs and treeless landscapes, that I found myself hiking completely nude one day. Well, not technically nude—I did have sandals and sunglasses on. But with all the boat traffic and clothed hikers and lack of foliage, I found a distinct lack of satyrism going on. Where was all the sex on the beach in great big groups of men that I had been promised?

I spotted a rock wall up away on the arid hillside, and a tan nude figure walking up to it. My cruising instincts directed me to follow him. I climbed up the slope and around the crumbling rock wall, and found a tall naked man in his forties with a shaved head. He must have been one of those Europeans who gets three months' vacation a year, judging by his deep-fried skin, and the lack of any visible tan lines on his gaunt body. He stood gazing out to the sea, one hand steadying himself on the rocks and another languidly stroking his long uncut shaft. He barely turned to me as I got down on one knee and began to assist him with his strokes, replacing his hand with my mouth. The man kept gazing out to the water, far beyond the horizon, like I wasn't there. Anyone passing by below could have seen us, there wasn't much coverage. But that kind of turned me on. My sunglasses became smudged as my face smushed his pubic hairs, and I took them off.

I felt his body shift, and I heard footsteps behind me. Before I could retract my face from the man's sweaty crotch, a random hand cupped one of my naked bent-over buttocks, and a finger casually slid up my unguarded ass crack. There must have been spit or olive oil or something on that finger, judging by how quickly it moistened the hair around my anus.

I looked up, and saw two men in swimsuits, their legs apart in a stance like a pose. One was tall and naturally brown and muscular and in his late forties, the other was pinkish and shorter and beefier and in his thirties. Their hands explored my exposed body in perfect unison, as a team, a unified wall of man flesh coming toward me glistening in the sun.

Keeping my position, I swiveled around to take the brown man's thick cock in my open mouth. It was so hefty, I nearly gagged. The pink man kept smacking my butt and playing with my hole, tapping it with the tips of his fingers. Before I knew it, I felt his cockhead at my entrance, pushing at my gate. The brown man held my shoulders, and I assumed the original gazing masturbator just kept on gazing.

After the pink cock had a few strokes, almost getting his whole erection into me, I heard the brown man say in accented English, "Give me a go." Again in perfect choreography, the two tagteamers spun me around until the brown dick was well inside of me, lubed up by something or another (maybe it was just sweat). He jammed his massive dick into me, and I let out a yelp. He slowed down, waiting for me to get used to its girth, which I never really did. No matter, he kept plowing my ass with his raw thickness as his friend grasped my shoulders in his arms, until I heard the accented voice ask me, "Yeah, you want that cum load, boy?"

It was a rhetorical question, since his sperm began pumping hot jets inside of me without skipping a beat. I had little choice but to take it all. I was now thankful my ass finally had a good amount of slick lubricant inside it, especially since the smaller but rock-hard pink cock went right in after. This one took longer to arrive at completion than his mate. He shoved his cock in harder and faster than his friend, and I was glad when I heard an American accent announce, "Here it cums. Take it fucker!" And I did.

By the time I was able to stand upright, the original gazing man was just finishing bringing his long roll of meat to a climax. A glob of his sperm hit me on my hairy leg and made a big white streak on my thigh. I felt another glob of someone's semen oozing down my leg from out of my ass, and in embarrassment I clenched my buttocks to make sure no more would escape.

"Thanks, guys," was all I could think to say (as if anything was needed to be said). I grabbed my sunglasses and scurried back down the hillside, clenching my buttocks all the way. I felt like a portable piece of meat on legs. I could make out the two men's hearty guffaws from behind the stone wall. I was surprised I didn't hear them smacking each other's palms in a triumphant high five.

Who were those pink and brown tag-team quasi-rapists? I had to admit, they knew exactly what they were doing.

I rushed back to my hotel and jerked off thinking about how it had all happened anonymously and all in broad daylight, like a porn fantasy. Like my satyr fantasy. Some childhood fantasies are worth the wait.

I spent the following days getting lost in the old town of Mykonos. It's a glorious stucco maze of intense whites and blues. Its walking streets curve this way and that, until you forget what direction you were originally heading to begin with. The town was purposely built to disorientate the invaders and pirates who frequented the place, and now shops and restaurants prey on confused tourists who lose their way in it. Eventually, one way or another, you're inevitably delivered to the edge of the Aegean Sea. It's here that you invariably sit at a wooden table and have a drink and watch the birds fly over postcard windmills. Day after day you get lost, but instead of ultimately mastering the quirks of the maze, the longer you stay in Mykonos, the more labyrinthine and mysterious it becomes. It slowly envelops you and shows you new revelations with every turn. It's changing and alive, it's moving. You surrender to it, knowing you will never get to the end of it all. And mystical Delos watches your moves from afar.

The salty summer nights in Mykonos never end, just as its summer days never cease to blaze. The winding pathways alternately widen and tighten and widen, and you jostle up next to tourists whose languages you can't identify. If you're lucky, you'll happen upon a small square that coaxes you into a lure where you think you will finally find your bearings.

I was lucky one night, since I not only stumbled upon a small square, but a square with a gay bar high above it called Icarus. I climbed the wooden stairs and entered a concave stucco cavern echoing with pulsing music. Not a soul was there, except a smiling bartender and a drag queen. It was 10:30 p.m. I should have known better. I had visited the tiny handful of gay clubs in Athens before midnight, only to be informed that no one shows up before 2 a.m., except other Americans.

The bartender was extremely handsome and smiling, and the drag queen was quick to notify me that he was straight and from Iran, of all places. ("Even though he calls himself *Persian*.") I didn't care if he was gay for pay, I flirted with him anyway. After one drink and hearing all about the drag queen's homeland of Belgium (why do travelers only tell you about the place they're from, not the place you're at?), I headed towards the door. I looked up and nearly bumped headfirst into the pink and brown tagteam couple. They both instantly recognized me, and smiled like two Cheshire cats.

"Hi," I said.

They mentioned their names and how this place was dead and how I should follow them to where the real action was. They seemed like they were almost frantically horny, on a search for the next orifice, wherever it might be. It was still early, so what the hell? I scurried along with them out of the square and down to the water and to the pier where the ferries dock during the day. At night, it was barren except for a few stray dogs under fuzzy streetlights. I followed the two of them into a pitch-black public bathroom. I had been there to take a piss that day, so the place wasn't totally foreign to me. I knew it was shaped like a long alley lined with urinals. But the shadowed panting figures all around me were something new.

I made my way into the crowded cottage, and felt random hands on my legs, buttocks, and torso, lifting my shirt. I kept my hand firmly in my front pocket, clutching my wallet for protection. As my eyes adjusted to the darkness, I could make out figures grinding, sucking, pants being unbuttoned, men on their knees. A lot of them seemed (or at least smelled) like Greek fisherman. They were here for a quick orgasm before they went off to bed, uncaring who or what gave it to them.

An older man swung me around and pressed himself against my back, yanking my trousers down and groping for my asshole. I was trying to keep my fingers on my wallet. I could feel the two tagteamers smiling at me in the dark close by.

Just as I felt the tip of the old man's erection penetrate me, I saw a flash of light outside. And then the sound of an engine. And then feet frantically shuffling about, and words muttered in Greek. Then the stern shouts of policemen.

I buttoned my jeans in a flash and grabbed hold of the brown tagteamer, who was tall and easy to spot. We emerged to find three or four uniformed police with flashlights striding towards the bathroom. The pink and brown couple knew what to do, and darted around the back of the building and then to one of the nearby entrances to the maze of old town. I followed them in hot pursuit. We walked briskly, rather than an all-out guilty run. I didn't glance behind me at the policemen, who seemed to be going toward the fishermen figures and not us.

Pink, brown, and I ducked into a tourist café, our faces flush with shame and excitement.

"Oh my god, I have never seen cops pull up there!" said the pink one.

"That was a close one," added the brown one.

I thanked them for saving my life and saving me a trip to Greek jail, which I assumed was as bad as Turkish jail à la *Midnight Express*. I bought the three of us a round of drinks. We all agreed that the police were not after us obvious tourists, and our weak rationalizations calmed our nerves.

After our drinks, we were laughing about the whole thing, and I could finally study the tagteamers' faces. They were both quite handsome, although I tried to hide the fact that the brown daddy (who was actually French) was much more my type. That's the eternal problem with threeways—it's nearly unfeasible to be attracted to two distinct humans with exact equality. The two men had been a couple for four years, they lived in Boston, they had been to Mykonos once before, and they were both self-identified "sluts" who had met at a sex party. And they enjoyed finding attractive victims like myself to feast on. (No surprise there.) I didn't doubt a word of what they were telling me. I was a bit envious—none of my boyfriends had ever been such a blatant partner in crime.

"That was pretty hot this afternoon at the beach," the pink one noted.

"I know. It was like a porn come to life. You guys just went for it. And you came a ton."

"We're not shy, as you can tell." They both winked. "C'mon. We're taking you back to our place to double fuck you."

Who was I to argue? I dutifully followed them. Although during the walk to their vacation villa, I wondered if they meant "double fuck" as in each tagteaming me back and forth individually, or "double fuck" as in two dicks inside of me at once? The brown cock was huge and thick enough on its own. And I had never been double fucked before. I began to worry about what I was getting myself into.

They stripped off my clothes the minute we got to their two-bedroom apartment. I was their specimen, their carnal banquet. Before I knew it, I had a dick inside me. "Damn, you got a nice hole. Get on top of me."

I did as I was told, and then felt another finger poking my asshole from behind.

"Listen, I've never been double fucked before, and I'm not sure I can take it all ..."

Before I could finish the sentence, another cockhead invaded its way into me, and a pair of arms bent me over so my butt cheeks were completely stretched and open to receive. I pushed back with my anal muscles, knowing that that would help me accept what they were shoving in me. They lathered their two cocks up with lube, and there I was, getting double fucked. It hurt, but I took it like a trooper (or at least a good guest).

Finally, one dick softened and withdrew, and the pink man left the room and returned with a camera in his hand.

"You can take pictures, but just don't get my face in them, please," I pleaded as I sat there impaled on the brown daddy dick.

"Don't worry," was the reply as the camera began clicking away. The brown cock's motions became more rapid, and I was thankful that my violated cavity would soon be accepting its reward of semen, signaling the end of the worst of the fucking.

Sure enough, brown French daddy loudly announced, "Take that fucking load up your hole." I guess that was his trademark phrase. I did, driving the cum deep into me, and the camera caught every gush. The two men seamlessly changed places, and the camera was there to catch every pump of the pink cock exploding inside me too.

The two grinned widely at each other, and I soon got the impression they would be up for round two in a few minutes. But my ass surely wouldn't be. I went to the toilet to empty myself of their creamy gifts and was relieved to see no blood in the bowl.

I took a deep breath, opened the door, put on my most dashing smile, and said, "You guys are really hot. Thanks for that! But I really gotta get back to my hotel."

They looked a little crestfallen, like their pound of flesh was escaping, but they allowed me to depart without a fuss. "I'll be walking funny for a week!" I laughed as I exited. It wasn't far from the truth.

During the next couple of nights, I was worried about casually bumping into the tagteam double fuckers again, since the maze of old town facilitated people stumbling upon one another over again and over again. Luckily for me and my anus, the tagteam was nowhere to be found. They were sexy, to be sure, but their one-two punch of unbridled sexual impetus (directly up my poor sore hole) was just too much to take. What about a kiss or a blow job? Was that too much to ask? Fucking for this tagteam was a contact sport—like rugby or Sumo wrestling. I'm sure their trail of victims spanned several cities and continents. In them, I had finally met my match.

I spent one evening wandering around the Mykonos maze trying to find a popular gay bar I had heard of but could never find. I turned a corner, and was greeted with a merry throng of men in tight shirts, completely blocking the lane. There was no point in trying to get through them, so I stood on the edge of them and peered in. Everyone was well and drunk, or on the cliff's edge of being dead drunk and ready to fall off. They conversed loudly in tight pockets of sunburned faces. I watched for awhile, and then decided just to go back the way I came. There wouldn't be a stray sheep in this crowd whom I could pick off and drag home. The flock was too thick.

As I walked away, a man walked towards me. He was tall and brown and French-looking, like the brown daddy tagteamer. It could have been his brother. This man in his forties wore a white button-up shirt and dress slacks and he looked a bit out of place. At first I thought he was some heterosexual who had taken an unknown gay turn down the maze. But his unbroken stare was unflinching. This brawny, strapping daddy had a bad case of the needing to get off, and bad.

As I passed him, he stopped and spoke to me. "Hi." An intense look.

"Hi."

We stood there for an awkward second. "You won't be able to get by up there," I advised. "The lane is totally packed."

"That's okay," he said in an accent I couldn't quite put my finger on. His mouth smiled, but his eyes didn't. "What are you up to?"

"Nothing. Why? What have you got in mind?"

"Taking you back to my place and getting you naked."

I smiled. "Sounds good to me."

I followed my new daddy out of the maze, to where his car was parked. We didn't say much in his concerted rush to scoop me up. His eagerness was sexy.

His car was a nice new Mercedes. It didn't look like a rental. "Where are you from?" I ventured. I hoped he wasn't a serial killer, or another tagteamer.

"I'm from Athens," he answered as his burly hand squeezed my leg. His fingers made their way up to my crotch, which was already hard. His vibe oozed raw masculinity. "I come to my home here on Mykonos on the weekends."

Nothing is too far away on tiny Mykonos, and we arrived at his villa in just a few minutes. I mentally kept track of where we were going, just in case I had to find my way home on my own. I could make out the lights of the old town twinkling across the small bay.

He flipped on the lights. The villa was no less than three stories tall. I guessed he was a shipping magnet or something—the only clichéd box I could place a rich Greek daddy into. He excused himself to go to the bathroom. I noticed photos of a wife and kids on the mantel in the living room.

"Your family?" I asked when he returned.

"Yes. They are in Athens. I come here alone to have fun." My straight radar was correct, after all. "Let's have some fun."

He pulled out a small baggie out of his pocket, and nonchalantly began lining neat rows of cocaine on the glass table. Oh, what the hell? I had already been double fucked, why not get high on coke in Mykonos as well? Fuck it. It might help my aching ass take what was sure to be his raring cock.

I tried to make it look like I knew what I was doing, tipping my head back after each snort, even though I had only ever done coke once or twice in my life. He soon took me and the baggie downstairs to the master suite. Its French windows perfectly overlooked the ocean. I felt like I was in a sales brochure for a luxury timeshare. Before I knew it, we were both naked on the sprawling bed, and I had his hairy circumcised cock in my mouth. He couldn't get hard right away, but I was sucking with the blind enthusiasm of a vacuum cleaner, high out of my mind. He was "straight" and horny and brown and hairy and hot and he was into me. Why is it so sexy when guys find you sexy?

He was only able to fuck me in short intervals between more lines, but I really didn't care. At that point, my asshole would be fine if it never saw another dick for a year or two. I just liked being in his huge masculine arms, imagining what his wife would think about all this—drugs and naked gay sex and bringing strange tourists back to their lovely vacation home.

When the sex wore off and the coke chatting began, I learned a lot about him. He told me about his three kids, how they all came down to Mykonos often during summer, how he had had the house for five years, how he liked fucking his wife. But that he liked fucking me more—which I loved to hear him say.

"In Greece, we always get married, no matter what we like to do in bed," he told me. "I can't do this in Athens, I know too many people there. So I come here without the family sometimes to have fun. Everyone has secrets, don't they?"

I thought about that one for awhile as I looked out of the French windows where the night sky began to crack with the coming light of another stark and sunny day. I didn't tell him too much about myself. I didn't tell him I had just been double fucked for the first time, I didn't tell him about the cops with flashlights chasing us out of the bathroom, I didn't tell him about my photos of the marble testicles of Dionysus. I didn't mention a lot of things.

Once the harsh dawn looked like she would truly rear her ugly head once and for all, he simply said, "Let me take you back to your hotel."

I tried to casually chat through my sleepless haze on the drive back. He was leaving that same day going back to Athens, and I could tell he was putting on his impersonal armor in preparation for the trip. He became cold and distant, and I didn't care. I had had a high night in a fabulous villa overlooking the Aegean Sea with a hot naked rich straightish Greek daddy. Never did find out what he did for a living, and who cared? He would soon be a vacation abstraction.

When I got back to my tiny hotel room, I tried to rinse the coke out of my nostrils, and I tried to sleep while the incessant sunshine blasted its way through the thin curtains. I tried to forget everything. But I couldn't.

My head ached for two days straight after that, and I couldn't stop the pain with ibuprofen or alcohol or sunbathing or sleep. My ass felt tender all over again, and my eyes couldn't handle the unstoppable blaring sun. I didn't want to go back down into the maze, I didn't want to bump into other people, I didn't want to feel a stranger's penis prodding my insides, I didn't want to see huge marble balls, and I didn't want to see a line of white powder in front of me ever again.

From the isolated perch of my hotel bed, I could look out the window past the balcony and make out the profile of the isle of Delos, the place where both sunshine and moonshine had been born. No wonder humans didn't live there any more—how could they when it's so close to the center of the galaxy? There's just too much energy, too much feeling, too much sun, too much history, too much of everything.

Damn you, you tempter Dionysus with your sweet wine and sweeter cock, spewing life-force all up into the far reaches of the universe. Goddamn you, goddamn you.

A Rescue and a Lost Prince in Tahiti

T
he flight attendant bent down and handed me a Diet Coke, smiling at me. There was a *tiare* flower behind his left ear, the delicate white symbol of French Polynesia. After all my years in Hawaii, I still couldn't remember if the flower behind the left ear meant he was already taken, or if it was the right. Or if anyone knew for sure. His equatorial skin was tan and deep and sensual against his appropriately sky blue uniform. His eyes, dark brown, as dark as unmapped volcanoes, lit up at me.

The plane would soon be landing in his remote isles thrown across the breadth of the great Pacific like splintered shards of discarded glass. Islands with no names, hard to get to and even harder to hold. I was on my way from Sydney to Papeete. It was a long-haul, long-protracted Air Tahiti Nui flight over the endless waters of the Earth. I was in a foul mood. Tom was still on my mind. I couldn't dislodge him. I had left him in Sydney a week ago, late at night, standing at his doorway, with hot raging tears in my eyes.

Tom, a semi-retarded American (at least a semi-retarded American *emotionally*), was the fateful catalyst for my long journey across this sea and sky in the first place. Tom was tall, in his early fifties, blond, and wealthy, and all those attributes were not gifts but curses. I had met him in New York City where I was living at the time. We had dated, and had had good sex. His cock was crooked and scarred where he once had to have it drained because of a recreational erection injection (the kind porn stars use) that had evidently lasted a bit too long. But the thing was thick and hefty, and he fucked me well with it, spraying his sperm deep and wide into me. Or I'd flip him over, and enter his milky white buttocks which were perfectly outlined with careful tan lines and pump him full of mine. We cuddled well too, despite the fact that in bed he wore a breathing mask apparatus over his face that was hooked up to a machine, for sleep apnea. It was like sleeping next to someone who was scuba diving.

There was something off about Tom, and if I had had my wits about me I would have sniffed the lingering whiff of expiration I could never quite put my finger on. He was like a carton of milk on the verge of going bad, but you go ahead drink it anyway. And then you get sick. Every time I thought I shouldn't be with him, he had a way of softening and showing his healthy whiteness, the part that hadn't gone bad yet. He had a way of bringing me back to him. He was a salesperson. The dark secret he was hiding was that his wealth had inflated his ego beyond all recognition, to the point where he supposed the laws of human physics didn't apply to him any more.

What do I mean? Let me vividly illustrate what bad human milk smells like. Tom and I had decided to rendezvous in Tahiti, and then we would fly to Sydney where he had a house and travel around Australia a bit. I arranged free hotels for us to stay in all along the way, comped to me in return for press coverage in my travel articles. I put Tom and myself up at the St. Regis resort in Bora Bora. It was one of those luxury wooden huts on stilts built over the see-through waters of a tropical lagoon, exactly like the postcards said they would. The jagged volcanic teeth of the Bora Bora mountain jut up behind, James Michener wrote long and hard about it all and it's one of the most romantic places in the universe. Did Tom kiss me or even hug me during our stay in Bora Bora? No. Did he try to obtain more free meals and drinks from the resort during our stay? Yes. Does he have more than enough money to treat me to the whole experience instead of me treating him? Yes. Was I a fool for not seeing all his selfish and shortsighted red flags slapping me across the face? Oh, yes.

Not convinced Tom had curdled yet? I'll skip over the time he screamed at me on the pier in Provincetown and fastforward to the moment we left Tahiti, when Tom strode up to the airline counter and upgraded himself to first class. Then he told me sorry, but he couldn't upgrade me since there were no more first class seats left. (Don't forget, I had just given him thousands of dollars worth of free hotel rooms.) I went up to the same counter person he had spoken with.

"Just wondering, do you guys have any more first class seats I can upgrade to?"

She looked at me without blinking. "Yes. We have several."

"Are you sure? My friend just told me you didn't."

"No, I just checked, and I'm quite sure we have several."

I fumed on the entire night flight to Sydney. How could Tom be such an asshole, and more importantly, how could I have not seen his assholeness clearly? The world was full of assholes, teeming with them like the underbelly of a starfish, but I was more concerned that I was a chump who accommodates them. Assholes can only expand into the space allowed around them.

If all that wasn't enough, Tom ordered me about his penthouse apartment overlooking the Sydney Opera House, demanding that I do chore after chore. I did a few, but when he finally said, "You're just using me for a nice place to stay in Sydney," it was the final straw.

I went online and found a cheap hotel by the airport and began packing my bags while he stared at me obliquely. It was nearly midnight when I had my bags in my hands and I kissed him on the forehead.

"Let's not do this to each other," I said softly. "I'm leaving."

"Well you just need to learn how to respect people!" he retorted.

"Tom, I hope you find someone who can give you what you need." The door shut behind me with a click.

I shook as I waited for the cab downstairs. The man behind the counter of Tom's luxury building gently asked if he could do anything for me. He seemed genuinely kind, and genuinely human. He watched me as I walked out of the glass doors and into the night.

All by myself, I took the two-week trip I had planned for Tom and myself across Queensland and the Northern Territories. Tom emailed me, begging for my forgiveness, but it was too late. I told him not to contact me, that I was blocking his emails, and he was not to call or try to show up anywhere on my trip. On the Ghan train from Darwin to Adelaide, I drank a whole bottle of champagne as I watched the nothingness of the Outback slip past me and let myself finally break down in the safety of a speeding cabin.

All this to show you the color of my state of being on my return flight back to Tahiti. I was a little less than human at that point. Ever since the night when I left Tom in Sydney, I had felt like a used punching bag, deflated and worn out. And jaded. And old.

And done. Well done. Burnt, even.

Which brings us to the pure innocence of a twenty-something flight attendant looking down at me with his robust eyes.

He was a complete package, with his lilting Tahitian accent sprinkled with French words, his graceful movements, his politeness. I asked him inane questions about his family, his hometown, his work. He answered all of them, punctuating each answer with a boyish giggle. We exchanged phone numbers, and he came over to my hotel the next evening. We took a long, warm shower as the clichéd tropical moon—as white and blaring as a police siren—blasted its way through my oceanfront suite. His kisses were long and free of agendas, and his wet naked body was open without trepidation. I sucked his rockhard and short brown cock as the shower water tried to drown me. My hands slid over his hairless body like canoes slipping across an empty ocean. I drank every drop of his sweet Tahitian nectar down my throat. His essence tasted exactly as it should: a mixture of pineapple and friendliness. I drank it like a thirsty person, swallowing each propulsion against the back of my throat. It filled my gut with its easy warmth. His form was honest against me, something I hadn't experienced in another body in a long, long while.

"When is your next flight?" I asked as we lay in my large bed with the windows open, the drapes slowly flapping in the breeze.

"I don't go back to work for a few days. What are you plans in Tahiti?"

"I am renting a car and driving around the island tomorrow."

"I can join you and show you my island."

The words were like a bad tourism commercial, but the feeling behind them couldn't have been more sincere. The next day, he showed me secret waterfalls plunging through the deep rainforest, muddy trails to spectacular vistas, and we laughed as we dined on fish at a beachfront restaurant while swatting flies away from our mouths. He even showed me the few dots that made up the small village where he grew up, pointing out houses and neighbors and churches and beaches. You could make out the faint outlines of other islands far away, ghosts watching us, quietly.

"This was my world. I didn't know anything else," he told me. I think he kind of wished he still lived in that cocoon, that he hadn't boarded planes and seen the rest of the world after all. I could see him as a small boy amid the scenery here, laughing and playing in his speck of land in the middle of the overwhelming ocean. I could see where he got his quiet peace from. I had spent enough time in tropical climates to divorce myself from the carefree islander mythical stereotype, but here he was right in front of me: calm, content, caring, and generous. Rich and green, like his island.

We made grand plans for him to visit me in the States, or for me to come back to Tahiti. He kissed me passionately in the parking lot where I dropped him off, in front of a small apartment complex where he lived with his grandmother. The nondescript building could have been anywhere, but here it was in the middle of the largest body of water on the planet. It floated there, like a bubble.

He wanted me to call him that evening so he could see me off and wave goodbye to me at the airport. I promised I would.

Later that night I tore my suite apart, trying to find the scrap of paper where he had written his name and phone number. I picked through every receipt, and then scoured the rental car for any small piece of trash I could find, under the seats, in the trunk. It was gone. And with it, he was gone too. I didn't even know his last name, and I wasn't sure which of the apartments he lived in.

I boarded the plane feeling awful, like I had committed the worst betrayal the island had ever seen. I would now be another heartless tourist who used him as an exotic way station, as a good story, a layover fling to be easily dismissed. He would think I had lied to him. His brow would furrow. He had in fact brought me back to life, renewed my faith in the kindness of strangers, that men could be loving and not cruel, that not everyone was operating from an ulterior motive.

When I got home I searched through everything in my luggage once again, but he was gone for good. Just the faint smell of brown skin and moonlight and an island far, far away.

When I told my friend about him, she told me perhaps he was an angel. And perhaps he was.

I hope that someday a kind man will board his flight and whisk him away on a loving adventure. That man will never lie to him or abuse him or let him down. He will tattoo his name and number on his heart never to be lost and my royal Tahitian will be treated like the true prince that he is.

A Moroccan Banana

My cousin and I were strolling through the main square in Fez, Morocco. He was one of the few people I knew who could upstage my own sexual sojourns. He was adjusting his trousers, having just returned from an exploit down a darkened corner and dead-end alleyway, where he had furiously masturbated a random man who had followed him there. My cousin was about forty, blond, short and beefy; he wore tight shirts and had a wandering eye. Especially for dark, surly, hairy young men—the type who seemed to naturally hunt him down and the type that Morocco was teeming with, great faceless herds of them.

I was a bit jealous of his brazenness, and also a bit scared. I told him he better watch it—he could easily be stabbed, robbed and left for dead in that dead end of an alley. I had waited patiently around the corner while he serviced the man, but I couldn't always be counted on to be on hand to save him.

"The guy followed me there," my cousin said in defense of his faux innocence.

"You can't tell anyone's motives here," I reprimanded. "Anything can happen." I had already told him about the British tourist who had been recently jailed for having sex with an eighteen-year-old Moroccan lad, and the local newspaper reporter who had been thrown in jail for writing about the minister of finance and his homosexual trysts at a Moroccan beach resort.

My cousin sighed. "The guy was just so hot. My God, he came so much."

I looked sideways at my handsome relative. Perhaps he had sucked the nameless man off, his raw knees on the cobblestone as the man's stained fingers went through his blond scalp and pushed his head on to his exploding cock, where my cousin swallowed every drop of the spicy sperm. Or perhaps my cousin had simply turned around, let the man roughly yank down his American jeans, spit in his hand, and shove his circumcised Muslim member into the offering of the soft pink hole until he ejaculated deep inside the foreigner with gruff satisfaction, my cousin's white freckled body pressed firmly up against a dark dirty wall, receiving every angry burst of the stranger's seed. Perhaps the man's cum was dripping down out of his butt as we walked.

I wish I could effortlessly receive Morocco the way my cousin did, but I was always a bit reticent here. My anus seemed to be perpetually clenched in Morocco. I had told my cousin to read Paul Bowles' novel *The Sheltering Sky* as required preparation for our trip. It was one of my all-time favorite books. In it, a world-weary post-war American couple is fatefully drawn deeper and deeper into the great emptiness of the North African desert, and they are never seen in the same form again. Perhaps I thought the same fate might be waiting for me and my cousin.

Morocco harbored something within it that could not to be completely trusted. It wasn't just because it was a Muslim country, or poor, or perfectly poised for exploiting tourists—God knows I'd been to plenty of places that fall into all three categories. It was something else, something not quite so quantifiable. We had already traveled through the cold, rock-strewn landscape that dominates Morocco with a tangible pressure. We had journeyed up into the High Atlas Mountains of legend, the thick harsh walls of the "Mountains of Mountains," as the local Berbers call them. The Atlas always stood quietly to one side, watching us. They were indeed holding up the sheltering sky.

We had briefly passed through the port city of Tangiers, the former site of the notorious International Zone (or "Interzone" à la *Naked Lunch*). Half a century earlier, this vacuum of lawlessness and no known sexual limits had attracted doomed queer characters on the edge of the world—Tennessee Williams, William Burroughs, Joe Orton, Allen Ginsberg, Paul Bowles. Alas, their days of sunny bohemia had long since been obliterated leaving no trace. The place was now dull, commercial, pragmatic—magicless.

Only the intrepid bisexual Bowles had remained in Tangiers for the long haul, from the 1950s until his death in 1999. And his ominous description of this luminous, numinous land kept echoing through my head:

"It was too powerful an entity not to lend itself to personification. The desert—its very silence was like tacit admission of the half-conscious presence it harbored."

Morocco was a sexual Venus fly trap, sweet and sticky but deadly and remorseless. No wonder sex tourists kept being drawn here, egged on by the words of long-dead poets and beatniks and by rumors of gay brothels that hadn't existed since the 1970s, if they had at all. Homosexuality is explicitly illegal in the kingdom of Morocco, regardless of the fact that the king himself is supposedly gay. His Big Brother-like portrait smiles down from nearly every store and office place in Morocco. He was handsome enough that I would do him. But I kept that to myself—you can be jailed for speaking ill of the monarch in any way, especially by calling him gay. The young Sidi Moulay Mohammed (Mohammed VI) ascended to the throne in 1999, but had been seen in more than one gay bar in Belgium when he studied there. Rumors of his royal cocksucking ways persist, despite his marriage to a woman.

But then, what is gay in the world of Morocco anyway? Gay is an abstraction, a luxurious aspiration in most parts of the globe. Well, gay *identity* is anyway. Most marriages in Morocco are arranged, women are cloistered away before marriage and men form strong emotional bonds with one another. The act of gay sex in Morocco, on the other hand, seems to have taken a permanent foothold like malaria, or tuberculosis.

Every man and boy, young and old, seemed to be eying my cousin and me in the square of Fez. Piercing gazes, stripping us to the bone. It wasn't just because we were foreigners—there were plenty of those. Or that they wanted our money—many shop owners' hollers made that clear as well. No, this was something more. Moroccan men in their long *jellaba* robes hid anything going on beneath their folds, the same way you couldn't tell what was going on behind the tall walls hiding the country's courtyards. There were no gay bars, gay hotels, or any kind of outwardly gay infrastructure in Morocco, but the explicitness of the public squares made up for it. They were cruisy in the most primal, anonymous way. Even the public baths—where men scrubbed each other clean wearing see-through underwear, their heavy testicles swaying to and fro under the suds—felt like sexless car washes compared to the seething meeting place of the square.

"Muslims don't have Christian guilt," an American architect once told me in Marrakech. "There are no categories of gay and straight." But the Moroccans to me weren't just Muslim—they were firmly Berber, Morocco's ancient non-Arab race of indigenous people. The Berbers had been a hard thorn in each of their conquerors' sides, be they Roman, Vandal, Arab, Spanish, or French. The ballsy Berber pride was on display in the squares, where young men strutted about in a cocky air that comes with centuries of hard-won freewill. You, the new invader Tourist, were simply another thing to be had, another thing to be fucked.

"Hello. What do you like to do?" My cousin and I looked down at the voice coming from a young boy walking alongside us in the square at Fez.

We stopped and stared at him for a moment. His clothes were clean, and he wore full-length trousers with his buttoned shirt neatly tucked in his waistband. He wore shoes, not sandals.

"What?" I said to the boy.

"Hello! What do you want? You like me?" He looked to be about twelve years old, maybe even eleven.

"What do you mean?" I asked. Did he even know what he was saying?

"I have a big banana!" he exclaimed. "You can have it for fifty U.S. dollars. One of you, or both of you." Evidently, he knew exactly what he was saying.

My cousin and I looked at each other. "How old are you?" he cousin demanded angrily.

"I am sixteen!"

We both laughed, than went quiet. "What are you doing here? Are you crazy? Do your parents know where you are?"

"Yes, they do. Come with me. Very big banana!" The youngster grabbed his crotch and squeezed.

"Where do your parents live? They let you do this?"

"They live in a village outside the city. But I take you to a room near here. It is safe."

"Are you kidding?" I asked. I looked around quickly. I didn't want to get arrested for even talking to the boy. "You shouldn't be doing this. You are too young!"

"I am sixteen I said!"

"I say you are about twelve. This is very dangerous for a young boy. And dangerous for us too. Your friends will probably rob us."

"Okay, I make it forty dollars for both of you." He grabbed my arm. "Come with me."

I jerked my arm away. "Listen, you should just go back to your village and stay away from this city. This is very dangerous. You will be killed. Go back to your parents."

He looked hurt at my words. "I send money to my parents, they are happy."

We stood and stared at him. He finally shrugged his shoulders in defeat.

"Okay, no banana for you then!"

The boy retreated back into the streets, into the masses, into the night. My cousin and I looked at each other, and I saw he suddenly felt ashamed for his prior alleyway behavior. We walked slowly back to the hotel in silence. It was the most disturbing evening we had in Morocco.

A Bathroom Wall on a New Zealand Beach

Beaches are innately erotic to me. It's not just the mystical meeting of land and water, the wet and the dry elements, the feeling of forever, achieved by setting your eyes on the inexorable horizon. It's probably something more carnal. Shirtless men in shorts, or better yet bikini briefs, or—best of all—completely nude, outdoors in nature as primitive beings, devoid of trappings, in their raw state in the sun and the wind. Add to that the mythical setting, and add to that a premise where strangers will gaze upon one another to fulfill their most basic desires. It's hard to imagine a more charged atmosphere for the sex drive in men.

My beach fetish began while I was working my way through puberty (the time when all fetishes are born). I was twelve to be exact. I had pubic hair, I was already jacking off, and I was well ahead of the game. I was acutely aware that I was gay, and I was pretty much okay with it. My mother had told me sex was natural, and I treated my cravings as such. I learned in school that in the past humans only lived to about forty years, so it made sense to me that my sex drive would begin to rev up a quarter of the way through my genetic life. And the taboo of desiring men only heightened everything for me, for the very reason that it was so forbidden.

I had a rudimentary concept of what being gay was, although I assumed it was a rare condition that only afflicted a small handful of men. Now it was just a matter of finding where that small handful was out there ...

So the day I tripped upon a copy of *The Advocate* at our local beach, complete with pictures of naked men bending over each other, doing whatever they were doing to one another, I thought I had struck the all-time mother lode stash of pornographic gold.

This beach was in Southern California, near the neighborhood where we lived. I'd often go down to the beach alone, to get away from my bitchy stepsisters. The dunes behind the beach had an arousing aura about them, and I would be drawn to walk there. As a child I could pick up on an atmosphere of dirtiness, the stench of sensuality. I could sense something sexual went on there. I almost feel it in my nostrils. I would explore the waves of sand, searching for some clue to my impulses. And slowly but surely, my juvenile instincts proved to be more correct than I could have ever imagined.

While exploring the dunes, I'd catch a random man lying on a towel wearing only a Speedo—something I'd rarely seen any man wear. ("Nut-huggers" the neighborhood boys mockingly called them.) I would carefully position myself on another dune and watch his glistening body through blades of grass. On subsequent visits to the dunes, I saw men tanning completely nude, and my young cock would nearly burst through the seams of my swim shorts. I never stopped to think why I never saw women in the dunes—I just assumed that men had the need to do these types of things while women didn't.

One time my excitement got the better of me, and I ventured too close to one naked man sunbathing. He spotted me spying on him, and quickly yanked back up his Speedo and tried to act like he didn't see me. But that one vision of his naked body and thick cock was enough to give me fodder for masturbation for days on end. I ran home and jacked off in the shower right afterwards—it was the only place I could cum without anyone else in the house knowing. I'd close my eyes tightly as the warm water fell over me, recalling the careful mental photograph of the men I'd seen in the dunes. Great globs of cum would erupt out of me like a volcano that I couldn't control, and I was vigilant in cleaning up each and every drop of sperm so my stepsisters wouldn't discover what I'd been doing.

In short, I was a pubescent boy who was already cruising beach dunes frequented by gay men. At twelve years of age. Spying on naked male flesh. Talk about a born pervert.

My sojourns through the dunes became a nearly daily occurrence. Sometimes I'd get lucky and spot a nude man or at least one in a bikini, and sometimes there was no one to be found. I got better and better at learning the best spots to find guys, and at what times of day, as well as how to better hide myself behind the wispy tops of the dunes.

On one late afternoon, my bare feet brushed against a newspaper half buried in the sand, in a cleft between two dunes. I dusted it off, held it up, and began thumbing through the crusty pages. I then saw the black and white pictures. One showed the back of a standing man's clenched buttocks. Another showed the front of a bulging jock strap. Another showed two men on top of each other, their faces twisted with pleasure—or was it exquisite pain? Either way, my heart was pounding in my chest and my boyhood rose almost straight out of my fly. I was clever enough to have the mind to methodically tear out each picture, including the men bending over on top of each other, which was the most mysterious yet intriguing photo of them all.

Just then, a figure appeared on another dune. He was wearing a small men's bikini. He stood and looked at me. I quickly sprang up from the newspaper, shamefully. I stuffed the torn pictures deep into my pockets. I turned and began walking in the opposite direction away from him, lest he see what I was doing and report me to the police or something. Or worse yet, to my parents.

As I walked away, I glanced back over my shoulder to see if the man was still looking at me. My second glance showed that he was now standing where I had left the newspaper. He had a beard and a trim, hairy torso. He stooped over to pick up the paper, then gingerly laid out his towel and began to read the torn pages. I was amazed and stopped to watch him from behind a dune. Then he peeled the bathing suit down off his hairy legs, and began to fondle himself. I had never seen anything like this before. I was so flustered and nervous at the vision that I began to walk away again. What if somebody saw him, or saw me looking at him? But I found myself glancing back over my shoulder once more, and this time the man spotted me. He smiled, holding his huge erection in his hand. Then he waved his arm, beckoning me back to him.

I nearly died. Everything was happening so fast. I had never seen a homosexual newspaper (I didn't know there were such things), let alone watch a man do in broad daylight what I secretly did in the shower every day. And to see both in such rapid succession was completely overwhelming. I kept walking away, periodically looking back. Now the man was on his back, his hard-on strong and wet in the sunshine. He was showing it to me. Excitement and fear spun inside my body. For a moment, I considered turning around and accepting his invitation. But I was too scared. I ended up walking slowly back home, unsure of what I should have done. When I got inside the safety of the shower, I saw the man lying there stroking his huge cock. Now I was kicking myself that I hadn't turned around to join him. It had been my one perfect opportunity to finally live out my fantasies in real life, and I blew it!

All that happened on a Sunday afternoon, and I returned to that same dune religiously on each subsequent Sunday thereafter in hopes of seeing the man again. But he was never to return. I did spy on other men sunbathing in the dunes, more mischievously now and a little more boldly. But none did what that bearded man had done. The only other event of note was seeing an old grandpa consciously hang his dick out of one side of his shorts at me as he briskly passed me on the beach.

The image of that bearded man lying on that towel with that glorious newspaper, the newspaper from another world, was burned forever in my mind. I tortured myself for years after considering what could have been, what should have been, what was mine to have if only I had seized it. What if I had gone towards him? Would my concepts of sex have been radically altered there on out? Would I have stopped having my homosexual feelings in response, like the quenching of a fire? Would it have made me an over-sexualized child, even an abused child? Would I have finally felt totally loved and needed by an adult stranger? I'll never know for sure how what that physical experience would have been, and things in life have a way of working themselves out for the better, regardless of what we desire at the time.

Four years later, I was a horny sixteen year old spending the Southern Hemisphere summer in New Zealand. My father was living on the North Island for a stint, and I was staying with him. I had procured an under-the-table job at the local beachside fish and chips takeaway, and I spent sweaty afternoons behind an apron as my skin glazed over with layers of fryer fat mist. The couple who owned the restaurant lived next door to it, and I'd often spend the night in their spare room rather than travel home. At night before I went to bed, I'd stroll along the beach and watch the moon and the headlights of the passing cars make designs in the water. Sometimes if there was no one around, I'd pull down my pants and jack off in the open air, my volleys of sperm landing with tiny little splashes in the water. Beaches just do that to me.

The beach also had a public restroom, and when I sat down on the toilet there one afternoon, I spotted a crude picture of a penis drawn on the back of the stall door. I leaned forward to decipher the writing next to it. A message implored the reader to leave a date and time for a session of cocksucking. I was intrigued by the caveman-like request. Next to it I penciled in the date after tomorrow, at midnight, after my shift was done. I said we'd meet in the bathroom. The next whole day I was on edge for the anonymous appointment to arrive, driving myself insane. What if a madman had written the note? What if it was a super ugly guy? What if he stabbed me or something? What if he never showed up? What had I done?

The next night, I quietly tiptoed out of the sliding glass door of my boss's house, hoping they didn't hear me. I strolled down the beach to the restrooms. No figures could be seen anywhere on the barren sand. The evening was lit by moonlight diffused through a thin filter of high clouds. I sat on the side of the road near the toilets, and waited. And waited. No one was there. After a half hour, my heart sank. I was ready to get up leave when I saw a human form making its way down the sand towards me. I got up and casually waltzed down to the water, and then in the direction of the figure. As we passed each other, I felt my arms shake.

"Have you got a light?" the figure asked.

"I don't smoke," I replied to the American-sounding voice.

We stood there for a moment in silence, and I could vaguely make out his features. He seemed relatively young and blond.

"Were you the guy who left the message?" the voice asked me.

"Yeah, I was." It sounded tough, but frail.

"I've got an RV around the corner ..."

"Uh, no." Being trapped in an RV sounded like a dangerous idea. "Um, let's walk down the beach," I suggested.

He complied, and we strolled along the beach in silence. It was then that I noticed another figure sitting on a picnic bench nearby.

"What's that guy doing there?" I muttered.

"He's a friend of mine. He might be interested in doing something too …" Oh great, now I would be killed by not one assailant, but two. It was probably easier to work as a team to dispose of the body and whatnot.

"Uh, look, maybe I should go …"

"No. Don't." The voice was friendly, almost pleading.

My heart was pumping so hard it felt like it was going to rip open my chest. "Then tell your friend to go. He needs to leave." I was proud how authoritative I sounded.

He looked at me in the dark. "Ok."

I watched his back retract into the night, and I could make out the two figures conversing, then the second figure walking away from us.

He returned to where he left me standing on the beach. "Are you sure you don't want to go to my RV?"

"No, I don't." I felt like I was losing control of the situation, even with the other guy now out of the picture. "Let's go down to the end of the cove," I ordered.

We walked along the beach past the front of the fish and chips shop and around a rocky point to a little cove. I now felt safe. I could see him better now. He was tall and thin, with shaggy blond hair that cascaded down his forehead. Maybe about twenty-five or twenty-six. When he took off his shorts, I could see a distinct bikini tan line. I took off my clothes too, and I felt his hairless body over me, sucking me and then me sucking him and both of us spewing cum all over each other in loud bursts under the moon. I was truly happy.

"Are you American?" he asked after we were done. We were kind of awkwardly lying in each other's arms, trying to be intimate but not too intimate.

"Yeah, from California. You?"

"I'm Canadian … Look, do you want to get together again?" he seemed eager.

"Sure." He seemed like he was okay. He didn't bite my dick off when he had it in his mouth or anything. "Do you work around here?"

"Yeah, down at the steakhouse in town."

I felt a little hiccup. The steakhouse was where my best friend Suzy was currently waiting tables. I didn't tell him that, though. "What do you do there?" I inquired.

"Do you really want to know?" He chuckled.

"Yeah, I do."

"I'm a stripper."

"Really?" That bit of information made the whole encounter ten times sexier in my eyes. Not only had a bagged a cute guy on my first foray into anonymous sex, I had bagged a male stripper to boot.

The following night, I rendezvoused with my Canadian stripper guy on the beach once again. It already felt like we were old friends. He suggested we go back to his RV once again, and I felt okay with the idea now. We walked through the little tourist beach town, all quiet and closed for the night. He assured me his friend who was on the bench last night was a cool guy, and I had nothing to be worried about. When we showed up to where the RV was parked by the side of a field, his friend stepped out of the vehicle and shook hands with me.

"I'm Darren." He was older than Chris, with dark hair and a bit more weight, but seemed to be friendly enough. However, his voice had an edge to it that I couldn't quite figure out. Having spent a lot of time around older people most of my life, I gauged him at around thirty-five years old. He was also from Canada.

The three of us sat on lawn chairs around a small campfire next to the RV and drank beer. Chris acted animated and excited at his new young discovery. I was excited too. I had heard about gay bars in Auckland and Wellington, but who knew there would actually be gay people in this small northern tourist corner of New Zealand.

"We're just traveling through," Darren explained to me. "Chris did some underwear modeling in Auckland, and now he's got this gig at the restaurant, so we'll probably stay here for awhile."

It wasn't long before Chris gave me a horny glance. "C'mon, let's go inside." I followed him up the stairs of the RV, and we sat on the bed. We began to undress each other and roll around on the mattress, and all the passion I had stored up for all my teenage years now seemed to spill across the sheets. Darren quietly opened the front door of RV and sat in the cabin, and I pretended I didn't notice him watching us through the curtains. I didn't really mind, I was just stoked to be finally getting some cock action! Chris tried to fuck me, but his long and smooth dick looked like it would split me in two. Instead, I held his cock in my hand and stroked it while he rubbed against my firm boy cheeks until his semen was smudged like an abstract painting all over my butt and back.

The next time I went over to Darren and Chris, it was also late at night. And once again, Darren jerked off in the front, spying on us through the curtains. I could hear him huff and puff as he came. I kind of liked him watching, it made me feel like a star attraction. But I wasn't attracted to Darren, and he knew it.

When I sneaked back in through the sliding glass door that night, my boss Yvonne was up. She asked me where I always went to at night, in as casual a voice as she could pretend. I told her I went for walks along the beach to clear my head, but both of us knew I was lying.

On the fifth or sixth night at the RV, Chris and I were inside sitting on the bed, chatting with Darren who was outside stoking the campfire. Just then, we heard footsteps. Darren rushed up and stood in front of the open door to the RV, using his body as a visual barricade so the visitor wouldn't see us inside. Chris quickly reached over and turned off the cabin light. Darren talked to the visitor as he slowly reached behind his back and closed the door behind him. Chris and I were fully clothed, but it was still a close call.

We could hear Darren outside. "Hi, Tristan. What's up?"

My ears couldn't believe they had heard that distinct name. Tristan was Suzy's boyfriend, a very cute boy about my age who was the fantasy of all the girls in town.

Chris and I cuddled up next to each other in the cabin, waiting for Tristan to leave. I finally whispered into his ear. "Does Tristan come over often?"

"Just to chat after work sometimes. That's all."

Hmm, I wondered about that.

As we sat in the dark, Chris began to nibble on my ear lobe. Then we began to kiss, slowly, quietly. It felt so good to be held by him. I had never had a girlfriend or boyfriend during my entire teenage youth, and I needed this. I liked kissing while still in our clothes and making love this way. We tried to be quiet, but I overheard Darren telling Tristan, "Oh, he's got a girl in there ..."

It was one long and protracted hour before Tristan finally left. Darren opened up the door.

"God, you guys were loud enough!" He was a bit pissed off.

"We weren't doing anything."

"Didn't sound like that from the outside!"

"Did he see anything through the door when he first showed up?"

"No. He just thought you had a girl in there and were trying to hide her."

I don't know why it took so long for it to dawn on me that Darren and Chris were together, as fulltime lovers, even though they were always careful to present each other as merely friends. It all became clear to me on subsequent visits to their RV, as Darren began to get bitchier and bitchier with me, telling me how Americans had fucked up the world and how they were all baby-killers and nuke-lovers. After a few visits, Darren all-out resented me. I tried to ignore his zingers and his tone and his jacking off sounds as he watched us through the curtains. I just concentrated on the blissful sex I was having with my hot tan stripper man Chris.

One morning, I knew when I walked into work that something was up. There was a weird look on Yvonne's face, like she had a fart that couldn't make its way out of her.

"There's something I need to tell you," she finally said to me in a low tone.

"What is it?"

"Well, it's difficult to say it." She wouldn't look me in the eyes.

My stomach felt like I had swallowed a large stone. I instantly knew it was something to do with me being gay. I knew it.

"Is my family ok? Has someone died?" I summoned up my best acting skills.

"No, no. Nothing like that ... it's about you."

"Well, then what is it?" I tried to wipe the countertops of the restaurant absentmindedly with a sponge.

"A friend of mine told me something yesterday."

"Yeah?"

"Well, she told me that you and that Canadian stripper bloke were having it on together. That you guys were lovers." Her cheeks were red.

I did not bat an eyelid. "Who told you that bullshit?"

"A friend."

"I'm sure. What a lie. Where did she hear it from?" I needed to know.

Yvonne's face lightened up. "I don't know. I'm sorry, but I had to ask. She told me because you were around our little son so much, so she had to tell me. You know, homosexuals carry a lot of diseases."

"Well, I hang around the guy, but that's it. We're just mates, that's all. I'm *not* his lover." My performance was quite convincing, even to me. The closet creates the best actors in the world.

"Oh, I know what it's like with people and rumors. I used to hang out with this married bloke and everyone thought we were bonking." She was speaking faster now, chatting and laughing. "I'm glad to know it's all just vicious gossip. What a relief!"

What if she did find out the truth? What if someone gave her proof about me and Chris? Would she and her husband awkwardly explain to me that the restaurant had slowed down and they wouldn't be able to keep me on as an employee? Would they be ashamed for me, embarrassed for me, distance themselves from me?

I racked my brain trying to figure out how the rumor started in the first place. It must have been Tristan that night at the caravan, less than a week ago. That was the only person who could have even remotely known I was with Chris that night. Had he caught a glimpse of us through the crack in the RV door?

The next day in town, I passed by Tristan and two other girls on the sidewalk. I casually said hello to them and walked quickly by. From behind my back, I swore I heard one of the girls say, "But he can't be gay. He doesn't look gay." Then I heard Tristan go, "Shhh."

I glanced over my shoulder, and they spun their heads away from me. My stomach sank to my knees. I quickened my pace to get home. Were people looking at me differently? I kept my head down and didn't look up at anyone. The small streets suddenly felt confining, unwelcoming, watching. I realized that if the rumors had already made their way to Yvonne, then everyone in town must know by now. I locked the sliding glass door behind me, and didn't go back into town for many days thereafter.

One overcast afternoon, I sat on the beach and ate some battered fish while watching the seagulls. I heard a voice behind me.

"Hey, sailor!"

I turned around, and it was Chris. He smiled and his blond hair fluttered in the breeze. He wore tight white shorts and suddenly looked so gay. At that moment, I felt nothing but hatred for him.

I scooped up my food and stood up. "I have to go."

His eyes squinted. "What's wrong?"

Did he have no clue what was going on in this microcosm of a village? "I'm just in a bad mood."

"Is it something I did?"

"No."

"Ok … Do you want to get together some time?"

"Look, I have to go, ok? See ya later," and I ran across the road. I felt like I might throw up my fish. His voice, his smooth face, his skinny arms, they all made me sick. Could he not see what a mockery he was?

The next time I saw Dad, I knew something was up. He was in one of his non-talkative, bitter moods. He drove me to work and once inside the car, he let me know exactly what was on his mind.

"One of the ladies at the general store took me aside yesterday and said, 'I'm sorry, but I have to tell you this, since it's been going around town. They're saying your son has been involved with some homos in town, and everyone knows.'" His voice was on the edge of eruption.

"That's not true."

"Look, I don't care how you want to live your life and with whom, but just don't involve me in it, ok!" The car swerved around a corner. "Don't you know how small these towns are? News like this gets around like wildfire! Couldn't you have been a little discreet when hanging out with your faggot friends? There are other people to consider! Did you ever wonder how this would affect my reputation? Did you?"

I didn't answer him. I just stared at the road ahead. He dropped me off at my boss's home, and I went inside and lay on the bed and felt like crying, but nothing came out.

I didn't talk much for the next couple of weeks. I hid behind the corner of the kitchen, out of the public view at the order counter. When I spotted any kids I knew, I ducked into the bathroom. I only ventured into town late at night. Once, I heard music coming from the steakhouse, and I peered in through the windows. I saw Chris prancing around in a black G-string, gyrating to the music while women hollered around him. I wanted to feel disgust at his brazen display of sickening gayness, but instead I was kind of turned on by the way his body moved, by his tan lines, by his smile. I missed having sex with him—this horrible object of my pain and my exile.

I sat inside the house and watched TV for days, while the summer morphed into a frigid and gray winter. The beach became threatening and the sea ominous and even the seagulls looked foreboding, their screeches were attack signals. I wondered if there was ever going to be a way out of this cold corner of New Zealand I was backed up into. Escape didn't seem plausible. It was too late. Everything had already happened. I had taken a chance, a glorious sexual risk via a message on a bathroom wall, and now I was paying for all the wanton pleasure of it. It was deserved retribution—nothing comes without its price. And my price was to be in the dark little house by myself, listening to the freezing waves push against the shore outside.

A Dying Cat in Hong Kong

I lived in Hong Kong for a couple of years in my early twenties. It was still a British colony then. This was before Red Chinese tanks rolled in to claim the expired lease on the place. There was little talk in the colony about things like human rights and voting and democracy, and no one cared. Not about such banal things. Not when there was money to be made. The sweatshops and junks of yore had acquiesced to glass and steel skyscrapers, and a man could be a janitor one week and a stockbroker in an Armani suit the next. The place was giddy with cash, flushed to the gills and tipsy with capitalism. The locals loved the feel of cold hard money in their hands, and they were good at making it. The city overflowed with wide-eyed optimism. At the time, it was also the gayest place in greater China.

But Hong Kong was far from rollickingly queer. It was fresh and modern and Western, and the inhabitants fancied themselves sophisticated and urbane, unlike those unwashed masses of rice paddy farmers across the border in Mainland China. This city was no Bangkok or Manila. There were no boy brothels with guys in underwear with numbers on them, or "macho dancer" strip bars with supple men soaping themselves up on shower stages. Barely a handful of gay bars could be found in Hong Kong, and most of those were tiny and more popular with foreigners than with the locals. The old sodomy law the British had established in 1865 (which carried a maximum sentence of life imprisonment) was not done away with until 1991. The Han Dynasty basked in open same-sex relationships, but that was way back in the time of the Roman Empire. Since then, Chairman Mao had made sure that homosexuals were labeled as "hooligans" and rounded up into re-education camps. Coming out as gay in Hong Kong remained a major loss of "face," and if you and your family lost any such face, you might as well kiss your honorable ass goodbye.

What closeted Hong Kong lacked in all things gay, it made up for with a clandestine forest of homo saunas dotted throughout the city. These little gay bathhouses were somehow crammed into converted apartment spaces that were hidden within towering high-rises. The saunas had oblique names like Babylon, Chaps, Rome Club, Gameboy. The Chinese jokingly referred to them as "rice steamers." They rarely even had a rainbow flag on their door—you had to make a concerted effort to even notice they existed. These establishments had no rooms for rent, just lockers, privacy booths, steam rooms, video rooms and full-sized bars within them. The shy Hong Kongers kept their long towels wrapped firmly around their waists as they drank glasses of whiskey and spent hours singing Canto Pop tunes to karaoke screens. Even though Hong Kong bars stayed open 'til the wee hours, the saunas politely closed up shop at midnight for some reason. I guess the guys couldn't stay out much later, or else their wives, parents or kids would begin to wonder about their whereabouts. If it weren't for the Japanese porn playing in a dark corner (there was no such thing as gay Chinese porn), you'd think the saunas had been built merely for friendly reunions. And they sort of were. They were the only places for the undercover gay population to escape their miniscule apartments jam-packed with other family members and go somewhere to let off some steam (as it were). These tranquil sanctuaries felt far away from the overcrowded, roller coaster of a city. Hong Kong's never-ending noise pollution resembled a bullet train derailing from its tracks, but inside the gay saunas, all you heard were the soothing sounds of warbling karaoke.

And it was in these establishments that I developed a complex about my attractiveness.

Photos from the era confirm I was young and cute. But I didn't feel that way at the time. The Chinese boys and men in the saunas would quickly look right past me, or worse yet, turn around and walk the other way. Sometimes briskly. In Cantonese, the word for foreigner is *gweilo*—which literally means "ghost man." That may not sound that bad, but for the Chinese, seeing a ghost or apparition brings immense bad luck upon you. I always chalked up the harsh reactions aimed at me in the saunas to the fact I was a living, walking, breathing "ghost man." But it still didn't make me feel any better about myself.

It was Edward who first suggested that my hair might be the issue. "We Chinese can be pretty racist. We think that hairy people with hairy bodies are further down on the evolutionary chain than we are. You know, like monkeys."

It all made sense: it was hirsute issues. I distinctly remember being in a sauna darkroom once, with hands gingerly reaching up to touch my torso but then quickly retracting in horror at the tactile sensation of bodily hair. It was like they had touched a hot stove or something. Sure, the Japanese and northern Chinese may sport some body hair, but not the smooth-as-silk Hong Kongers. They had been gawking at me in my towel like I was a Neolithic specimen from another epoch.

I met Edward floating down a hallway of one of the saunas. He smiled widely at me as I passed by him, and I was taken aback. The he followed me around like a lost puppy dog. He was a couple years younger with a small frame and deep eyes and a nicely curved tush. As expected, barely a hair could be found on his thin body. He cornered me in the steam room, and I was surprised when he yanked my towel open and boldly went right down on my white hairy cock while another guy watched speechlessly. Hong Kongers save that kind of behavior for rooms with locked doors, thank you very much! I came what felt like a couple of liters of semen, and Edward gulped it all gladly down his throat. Let's just say he wasn't your typically modest Chinese boy.

"I lived in England for awhile, and I guess that's where I became a potato queen," Edward told me in his clipped yet rubbery Chinese/British hybrid accent. He was the first person to turn me on to the term *potato queen*. I knew about rice queens, but had no idea of this polar opposite—Asian guys who are into Caucasian guys.

Edward was a welcome relief to my young ego. At least I now understand how ethnicities in my own country could be bruised by racially-fueled low self esteem. "You are so handsome, I think you are beautiful," he would say over and over again. Maybe that's why I liked having Edward around. I grew up around people telling me I was stupid and ugly, and his vision of me was pure and full of light.

Edward would go to the trouble of taking the metro and a long double-decker bus ride to visit me in the rural New Territories, something none of my other friends from the city ever did. I lived away from the thick hustle of the skyscrapers, in an area where verdant hills cascaded into lonely bays punctuated by rocky islets. It was the China of an old painting, and on long hikes I would stumble across lone circular hillside graves where the views of the ocean were superb and thus the deceased enjoyed the proper *feng shui* for a peaceful eternal rest. I thought this whole countryside enjoyed good *feng shui*, but it was something I couldn't convince my city friends of. You got the feeling Hong Kongers weren't comfortable being that far away from cement. But Edward was a different breed of Hong Konger.

"I like your kitten," Edward said on his first visit to my flat, as he scooped up my gray kitty from the tiled floor. He held the animal up to his face and closed his eyes, listening to it softly purr. I had never seen a local with such a tender spot for cats—most just seemed to throw rocks at them. Edward kissed her head, and then gently placed the kitten down before crossing the room and kissing me firmly on the lips. We lay down on my small bed, his smooth body pinned underneath the coarseness of my chest hair, our mouths locked together without breathing. I slowly pushed down his clothes and entered his hairless hole using just saliva as lubricant, and he didn't stop me as I soon ejaculated deep inside of him. "I knew you would do that," he whispered in my ear while my hard cock was bathed in semen inside his boyish ass. "And I was hoping you would."

One day while I was on the phone to Edward, a loud splash came from the bathroom. I had been filling the tub when he called, and I rushed in to find my kitten struggling to get out of the boiling water. I tried to fish her out, burning my hands. I grabbed a towel and scooped her out. Her wet body bolted under the couch. I grabbed her, and watched as puffy white welts and blisters began to form over her face and paws.

"I'll have to call you back, Edward. The cat just fell into some very hot water and I think it's really bad."

Edward gasped. "I'm coming over."

When he entered an hour later, I showed Edward the shaking kitten wrapped up in a blanket. She was emitting a deep moan. Edward scooped her up once again, and I watched as he gently cradled the kitten, tears working their way down his cheeks. I had rarely seen a man show so much emotion so effortlessly. He cried for some time before the creature slowly died in his arms.

Edward and I spent that evening in my bed, naked, pressing against each other. A lightening storm was brewing outside, with claps of thunder that felt like earthquakes and cracked like whips above the house. But it was okay. His tenderness was overwhelming and all encompassing, and to this day I don't know if I've met a stranger in an unknown land who has given of himself so fluently and selflessly.

That Plane to Cape Town

I t was a tipsy night in Cape Town. My gay tour group and I sat at long wooden tables amid laughing candlelight that licked up at our faces, as we sipped and then gulped fine South African wines. The restaurant was snug and stucco and historic, and the night outside was chilled by the South Atlantic Ocean. Even though the seats were hard under our asses, no one wanted to get up and leave. With the candles dancing, the wine flowing, and the smiling eyes of the gay Cape Tonian locals sitting across from us, it was a gloriously clichéd enchanted African evening.

I was sitting across from an Afrikaner named Reinard. His name sounded harsher than he was. He spoke English perfectly, but with a slight Dutch accent. Or was it African? His accent was clipped and pulled back, like he was trying to gargle and swallow his thoughts at the same time. But he himself was not pulled back. His long, lanky fingers touched mine frequently across the planks of the wooden table, his tall forehead looming masculine and distinguished in the dim yellow light. He worked as a local radio personality. His dark dinner jacket gave him an air of impressive authority, and it underscored the warmth and openness of his character. Why, oh why, do Americans spend so much time trying to project an idea of who they think they are, or how they want people to perceive them, when there is nothing sexier than someone who is calm and comfortable in their own natural skin?

Reinard and I conversed long through that dark, long, refrigerated night. We spoke about politics, about how Afrikaners (the descendents of Dutch settlers) had screwed up the country and held it hostage from the world for so long under apartheid (an Afrikaans word). He told me how gay Cape Town was, with its brothels and bars and cruising, but how it was also violently homophobic and sometimes menacing. He was brutally honest and direct, and charmingly so. Nothing was hidden—he was as wise as a saint, and as innocent as a newborn. Reinard would not take his darting eyes or fingers off me. They kept coming back to me like they were reading Braille. We eventually ended up in his cool bed in the old Green Point neighborhood, where the cobblestone streets wandered aimlessly about trying to find where they were going to.

He was naked on top of me with his lankiness, kissing me thirstily, like I was a commodity in short supply. His foreskin was long and brushed against my stomach, a snail's trail of precum forming up and down my torso. When he ejaculated, the cum got trapped in the bouquet of foreskin. Even when he closed his eyes to orgasm, it wasn't an inward act of selfishness, but an ecstatic gesture of romance, like he was savoring a flavor between us. I lay in his arms for a long time that night, and listened to voices on the streets outside. I could feel his nostrils spread his sweet breath over my hairy chest, parting each follicle like a mountain breeze through a dense forest.

In the dark, I pictured myself walking these ancient streets under the looming mesa of Table Mountain high above me, and coming home to this tall, brown-eyed, white-skinned man who would devour me every night like a good meal while I never tired of his mysterious withdrawn accent.

I obediently followed my tour group as it departed South Africa for Botswana, and left Reinard alone in Cape Town. I thought I had at least given him an exotic night of love American style, but his deep eyes were too pure and unadulterated to see me as a passing tourist. They pierced through me as I said goodbye to him. I felt guilty, like I was leaving a pet at an animal shelter.

Once I returned to the States, Reinard sent me a number of emails.

In fact, he emailed me for ten years.

And he still emails me. Sometimes Reinard and I go for months without any correspondence, but through our fledgling electronic affair transmitted across time and space, I know Reinard better than many of my geographically-proximate friends. Neither of us says a whole lot, but we both know there was something there in our brief night together.

I never returned to South Africa.

What if I had? What if I had the balls to follow my heart to the ends of the Earth, crossing oceans and hemispheres and meridians, to watch Reinard come home every night and greet me in his pulled-back accent? Night after night, lying in bed with the voices outside, would we ever show each other to be the mere humans we were? Would the pipedream collapse, and fights over unpaid bills and dirty dishes and petty jealousies and work and time and place begin to flood our little boat until we were underwater? Would that greatest cancer of all—bitterness—seep into our reality and eat away at anything that could have possibly been good between us?

And would my fear of bad endings diffuse what could—and possibly, should—have been?

Life has so many possible paths, yet we focus our minds on just one road, like it's all somehow preordained. Even visiting Cape Town to see Reinard seemed impractical and expensive and silly, so I never did. But the world is huge, and he and I kept emailing each other like it would all eventually happen.

Years passed, and all I have in front of me are a collection of failed relationships and dating attempts that have left me with a few good friends and many near-misses. One thought has always percolated through the back of my mind: that I was instead "supposed" to be with Reinard, and that I had somehow missed that train without ever realizing I was supposed to be on it.

But how was I to know what my true life really looked like, where I was really meant to be on this Earth? Time is always leaving us without us even knowing, reeling backwards from us in an expanding universe. Ten years can go by in a second. Maybe one day in the near or distant or dim future, I will just get on that plane to Cape Town and finally live my true life.

A Parked Car in Palm Springs

The sun was setting in Palm Springs, turning the mountains pink. It would be dark soon.

I got on the Internet, and right away I received an email from Adam. He was twenty-six, and we had hooked up a few months earlier and had randomly played online tag since. He wanted to see me, now.

I picked him up from his friend's place, and took him to mine. The last shoots of daylight drizzled in through the huge windows of my bedroom, and the desert night sat quietly beyond, patiently waiting to engulf us in a deluge. We kissed, I think for the first time, and he pressed his body so close to mine it almost hurt. He was so much thinner and smaller and more defenseless than I remembered. His smooth Latin skin grated up against my hairy torso like it wanted to be scrubbed clean of something.

We stayed like this for a while, not so much having sex as just clinging on to each other, breathing. Eventually, his phone rang. He hopped up. I now remembered his phone was always ringing, there was always some other plan on the horizon, some other formless idea of what to do with the coming hours.

"You wanna go over to my friend's place? He lives at this gay clothing optional apartment complex."

"Hmmm ... sounds interesting."

We buzzed the bell at the wooden gate, and his friend Dean answered, albeit fully clothed. I strolled around the complex and barely saw a soul. It was the remains of what used to be a gay resort, but this wasn't the free-for-all party my inquiring mind had anticipated. But then it never is, is it?

Dean made us drinks in his modest one-bedroom apartment while we watched bad porn and made various criticisms about it. Neighbors popped their heads in and joined us, not seeming to stay very long. Finally, Adam's phone rang again. It was time to go off somewhere else, to pour ourselves into the unknown night.

"Mind if we stop by my car?" I pulled up behind his parked four-door. He popped the trunk open and it was overflowing with clothes and belongings that almost spilled on to the ground. It was his makeshift house.

"You got a place to stay, right?" I asked him when he got back into my car.

"Yeah, at my friend's. But most of my stuff is in my car."

"I lived in my car for a few weeks in college when I was in-between places, so I know how it is." I tried to smile.

He looked at my sheepishly. "There have been some nights that I have slept in my car." He held up a bright orange ticket in his hand and read it. "They may tow the car. It's been parked here too long. But I got a day or two to move it. Just need to get my friend with the jumper cables to start it up first."

The next stop was his friend's motel room. An older guy sat on the bed while a younger guy obsessively checked his iPhone. The air was thick as fog with some kind of mixture of smoke from God knew what. I could barely breathe. I asked if I could open the door to let air in. I was glad when Adam soon announced we had to go.

"I can walk home from here," he told me in the motel parking lot. He was holding back the water in his eyes. "I'm sorry. I'm such a mess."

"What do you mean?" I hugged him. I felt he would fight anything I tried to give him with every atom of his being.

"Thanks for putting up with me tonight." He pushed himself away, unlocking me. "Call me later, like in an hour or so."

"Why?" I asked. It came out wrong.

"Fine. Don't." His figure walked away from me across the dark parking lot. I could only make out the shape of his light pants. He would disappear into the vague nighttime like a dim star obscured by an unseen cloud, and that would be the last visible trace of him.

I thought about just letting his chaotic life, his monumental mess, go. It wasn't worth it. His muddled existence was his own. But as I turned out of the parking lot, I found myself nearing his parked car. He was fishing something out of the back seat. I rolled down my window.

"Are you going to be okay?"

"I hope so," was his honest reply.

Antarctica and Icy Hearts

When I told my friends I was going to Antarctica, everyone just looked at me strangely, except for my photographer friend Luke who told me flat out, "I'm going with you."

"I don't know, I'll have to see," I backpedalled.

I wasn't sure if I wanted to share this intense experience with anyone, and although Luke and I had screwed around a bit together, his neediness rubbed my independent streak the wrong way. I'm closer to the world when traveling without another buffer-person. But I pictured myself having dinner alone every night on the ship with a hundred other strangers, and bringing Luke along suddenly sounded better. I've only ever felt alone in a group of people anyway.

We boarded our 400-foot Russian ice vessel in a far-flung village at the southernmost tip of South America. Signs everywhere stated "El Fin del Mundo," like a warning. We hung on to the chilly decks watching the land retract from us, as small chunks of ice appeared in the water and huge glider-like albatross birds ominously flew above them. "My God, the Earth is huge," Luke finally stated, his voice a little nervous. "I'm glad you brought me here." He leaned against me and gave me a hug. I hugged back, but not too hard.

That night as the icy waves thrashed against our porthole, Luke snuggled in the narrow bed next to me, his constant erection pressed on my leg, keeping me company. He was excited to be going to Antarctica, excited to be with me.

The first sight of Antarctica was brownie-colored mountains smothered in a thick coating of frosting rising from bays filled with ice sculptures. I signed up for the kayaking excursions, and Luke was miffed. "I thought you were going to help me take pictures and help with my equipment."

"I'm sorry. I already signed up." I wasn't going to miss the chance to kayak in Antarctica, no matter what. "Listen, I can make time to help you too."

"Ok, whatever."

As I kayaked around the bay encircled by white mountains, I spotted Luke setting up his huge camera on the dark rocks next to a penguin rookery. I waved. He barely waved back, turning around from me. I tried to focus on how mind-boggling it was that I was actually here on this frozen planet within a planet, and not on Luke's mood. This was precisely why I hated traveling with someone else, absorbing their feelings instead of the true energy of the place. That damn camera, that big bulky thing that couldn't be moved by just one person, it was our whole weird relationship.

"How long have you and Luke been together?" one of the pleasant Australian passengers asked me.

"We aren't boyfriends," I answered looking down, a little embarrassed.

"Really? You seem so close together."

"I think Luke would like us to be. But I don't really want that. I was with a guy for ten years before. I don't really want a boyfriend right now."

"You just seem like boyfriends to me."

I wish it were as easy as she made it sound. I wish Luke and I could have loved each other without any expectations or explanations. But what I needed was the great world and the unknown lands. In some egotistical way, I wanted to be Antarctica herself. I wanted to be the land no one could own.

A photographer on one of the first ill-fated early 1900s ship explorations of Antarctica, when the whole crew was shipwrecked only to return to conscription into World War I, summed it up in his journal: "Life is one long call to conflict, anyway."

On the plane ride home, Luke and I reminisced about the whole otherworldly experience. We felt like we were returning to the planet in a space ship.

"It was really special what we just did. Thank you so much." He genuinely meant it.

His warmth momentarily melted my icy heart, and I gazed into his eyes. I could almost see the continents within. I squeezed his arm and thought about holding his hand between our seats, clutching it all the way home.

But I didn't.

Perhaps love is one long call to conflict as well.

A Drunken Taxi Ride Through the Magic Kingdom of Orlando

A sea of telltale red shirts flooded the muggy, tropical streets of The Happiest Place on Earth. Throngs of sweaty gays and lesbians chanted *"Diva! Diva!"* in perfect unison at the top of their lungs as Cruella de Vil floated by in the midday parade. She struck poses and vamped it up for the queer sea of red. A hunky Aladdin tried hard not to bust up laughing at the catcalls and wolf whistles hurled at him as he floated past atop his magic carpet. Bitchy comments we also thrown at Cinderella's stepsisters passing by. Her castle towered in the distance, deep in the swampy inlands of Florida where the magical kingdom of Disney World lived.

I pitied any clueless straight family who naively chose this date, the first Saturday in June, to bring their children here. God help those poor unfortunate nuclear families who had saved up their money and had driven all the way from Alabama and Arkansas to Florida, along miles of ugly motor ways through the nondescript mini-mall wasteland that is mainstream America. All that, only to be greeted by a nightmarishly queer red river of uninhibited mouse-eared LGBT revelers. The poor heterosexuals were most certainly blissfully unaware of the gay bedlam of unrestrained high-pitched delight that was in store for them. I'm sure the parents would ignore it all at first, pretending it wasn't really happening. Think of the children! But then they would become slowly overwhelmed by the deluge of homosexuals swirling all around them, and chubby little Suzy would begin to ask awkward questions, and Mom would have to somehow address what had happened to their freshly-scrubbed G-rated park. Dad would hem and haw and eventually mutter some oblique things about "those people being different from us." Suzy would stare at the two girls who dressed like boys and kissed each other with pierced tongues, and little Timmy would soon pick up on all the finger snapping and random celebrity references he was overhearing. And then perhaps Timmy would look around and say to himself with a sigh of deep relief, "Thank you, God. There *is* a truly fabulous future waiting for me after all!"

Gay Days at Disney World began in the early 1990s as a coordinated effort for a whole bunch of gays and lesbians and their ilk to show up wearing red T-shirts to make their presence felt. It began with just a few hundred brave souls. Now, twenty years later, well over 150,000 limpwristers and rugmunchers arrived for a six-day smorgasbord extravaganza of events throughout Orlando's array of theme parks. Disney World never officially endorsed the event, lest they incur the wrath of the region's Bible Belters who have threatened to boycott Orlando more than once over the specter of Gay Days. But the red tide of queers keeps washing up here with the annual consistency of a celestial occurrence. Just try to keep gays away from something as magical as Disney World!

I went to my first Gay Days with my friend Ted, who was a nerd just like me. Without irony, we said hi to Mary Poppins and Alice in Wonderland in the lobby of our Victorian-style hotel (which of course was designed to only appear old). Once in our room, amidst flowered wallpaper festooned with little mouse ears, we carefully mapped out our day with in the Magical Kingdom, meticulously circling all the must-dos and timing it all so we could visit neighboring Epcot as well. Once in the park, we systematically hit all the important rides first: *It's a Small World, The Haunted Mansion,* and *Pirates of the Caribbean.* We made profound pronouncements on the quality of each like we were sommeliers rating fine wines.

Ted got me, and I got him. We got along like the best of brothers. We had met through a mutual friend in New York, and we fucked each other a couple of times in a casual get-to-know-you gay-handshake kind of way. Together we attended The Night of a Thousand Stevies in Manhattan, that legendary Stevie Nicks tribute party that billed itself as a "riot of swirling lace and tambourines." We both dressed as hippy cowboys in plaid shirts draped with beaded necklaces and topped with ten-gallon hats. Once inside, we were soon properly hammered. Then Ted began to aggressively French kiss me like he was a drowning man and my face was full of oxygen. I was taken aback. I was pretty sure we hadn't ever kissed that way before, even when we were having sex. We had always merely been buds hanging out together. So I wasn't expecting my heart to jump out of my rib cage as his face drew close to mine. But it did. My hand found the crook of Ted's lower back, and I felt it arch as he pulled himself closer to me. With one hand he held the back of my head so he could push his tongue deeper into my open mouth. My cock was so hard in my tight cowboy jeans, I thought it would explode just from his torso rubbing against mine.

"Wow, I never knew I was so turned on by cowboys," Ted remarked as he pulled away for a breath, his eyes twinkling at me while *Stand Back* blared in the background. "Maybe we should be seeing each other more often," he said. I smiled at him. Then we continued our drunken-breath make-out session for another two whole hours until the last swirl of lace and the final jangle of the tambourine at last subsided.

I guess the most erotic moments in life are the ones that are least expected. And they're certainly the most romantic.

We were too wasted that night to have sex again, but we went out for drinks later that week. We boarded the train for New York's deep dark boroughs, and in Jackson Heights we explored Latin gay bars and Spanish-speaking tranny dives. Ted and I were both drawn to a similar flavor of men: ethnic, swarthy, a little rough around the edges, but sweet with puppy eyes. Ted wasn't my typical type. He was so Waspy white bread Caucasian that our friends referred to him as the Blue Boy. You could almost make out his veins pulsating beneath his translucent skin, like a pale vampire. His hair was a dark auburn, a color I had never warmed up to, having grown up with temperamental redheads in my own family. Then why did my eyes keep darting away from the tasty toasty-brown Mexican and Puerto Rican boys in the bars, and back to the blue coldness of Ted? Why did my hands want to go back to the soft arch of his lower back? Why did my arm want to drape itself across his shoulder? We were just buds, I knew that. But I wanted him to pull my head towards his tongue like he had done the other night. I wanted to taste him again.

The evening ended disappointingly sober. On the empty and overly fluorescent train ride back to Manhattan, I made a passing reference to what Ted had said the other night, about how we should hang out more together. I probably made some clumsy joke about it being like us dating. My voice was straining to sound casual, but that stupid heart was beating hard through my ribs once again.

Ted sat slumped in the seat and lazily looked out the window at the black tunnel through the train's scratched windows. "Yeah, I dunno. I guess I'm not really feeling it." He yawned.

My heart stopped pounding, and my breath became slower.

I stayed angry at Ted for a couple of days, telling myself I wasn't. It was all so pointless. I was my own torturer. Ted had just been casually honest. What else did I expect from one night of drunken kissing fueled by Fleetwood Mac songs? I had been too inept to explain how I really felt anyway, and he just assumed we were buds. The one thing I know about life is that you can't really fight against it. My fantasy about Ted and me as some sort of couple would in reality probably have been a silly disaster. You don't know you actually dodged a bullet due to the very fact that it didn't hit you. The same holds true about things like missed flights. Perhaps that airplane would have crashed, who knows? Maybe the universe is actually looking after us in ways we completely don't see. The hidden booby traps of life only reveal themselves years later, if at all, and sometimes we don't know how incredibly lucky we are.

At least that's what I told myself about Ted. I rarely got schoolgirl crushes like that. I felt like a fool.

By the time Gay Days came around, I was well over Ted and had forgiven him in my own mind. It had been over a year since that fateful Night of a Thousand Stevies, and we were simply buddies. I loved him as a friend. But every now and then a backhanded remark or veiled put-down came out of my mouth hurled in his direction, and the tone would surprise me when it hit the open air. Some sort of reservoir of hurt and anger about Ted still lingered somewhere inside me, and I made a conscious effort to drain it until it was bone dry.

"As a kid at Disneyland, I never thought I'd see the day where every fucking person in line around me is a cocksucker," I remarked. Ted cracked up. I loved watching him laugh at my stupid jokes. Behind us, a couple of queens in red designer shirts and gaudy rainbow necklaces hollered back, "We're not just cocksuckers. We're asseaters too, bitch!"

Ted listened intently to my nerdy lectures about the history of the Disney theme parks, about how my cousins lived just down the freeway from Disneyland in California. I told him how my oldest cousin Dan worked as the tall, dumb bear mascot from the country jamboree. I told him how the park hid a maze of underground tunnels the staff used to traverse the park. I told him how employees were issued official underwear to wear under their costumes and how they were not allowed to wear their own. I tried to impress him. Sometimes I think I did.

"Was there any making out on *Small World*?" Lisa winked at me as we downed another vodka and cranberry inside her generic Ramada hotel room. Baby dykes in tank tops filled her suite, orbiting around Lisa's tall blonde frame like a lesbian May Pole. She knew all about Ted and me and The Night of a Thousand Stevies.

"The queens in the boats were too busy singing along to those creepy puppet robot things. Me and Ted did too."

"Really? I would have thought you guys would be using your mouths to do other things!" She winked again.

"Gays having sex inside *It's a Small World* is like Catholics having sex inside a church."

Ted came up to us and lurched forward and gave me a tipsy kiss on the cheek. Lisa's eyebrows raised up on to her forehead. He handed me a glass of pure vodka.

"Uh, isn't there supposed to be some juice in this?" I asked. His glazed-over eyes stared through me, like that night we had made out. Lesbian hoots and hollers echoed from the balcony, and the heavy and humid sky beyond was ready to explode with rain.

"I think it's time to take Ted home," Lisa finally suggested a little later as she began to lie her body in an unformed tipsy heap on the bed. Cute young dykes dissipated out of the room. All the vodka bottles were completely empty.

I held Ted's arm as we staggered into a cab and landed in a pile in the backseat, his torso splayed out across mine. We blurted out our hotel name, and I felt myself beginning to pass out. Ted started to snore. But the cabbie was curiously chatty.

"Are you guys in Orlando for a special event?"

"Uh huh," I answered.

"The gay event going on?"

"That's the one ..."

"Oh, very good." I could see the outline of a human smile in the rearview mirror, but my eyes couldn't really keep focused on it. There was some sort of dark and handsome Middle Eastern face attached to a nodding head staring at our dead drunk carcasses overlapped across the backseat.

My travels around the world have trained me to be aware of where I am and what's happening, even through the heavy curtain of drunkenness. So I periodically lifted my head up to the window and tried to recognize landmarks to make sure the driver wasn't taking us into the swamps to dispose of our bodies or something. Why else would he be staring at us and smiling?

The cab at last pulled up to our fake Victorian hotel. It looked even cheesier than I remembered. I threw some cash into the driver's hand. His head was now completely turned towards us, and it kept grinning at Ted and me. Its smile wouldn't stop. He was a Cheshire Cat.

I tried to push Ted's listless body out the door. I looked up again at the driver, and the smile was still fixed upon us, like a portrait with eyes that follow you around the room. But it felt genuinely friendly enough, and it was totally interested in the two bodies attempting to dislodge themselves out of his backseat.

"Perhaps you guys would like some company up in your room?" The cat grinned again. I was transfixed, I couldn't say no. It sounded like he wanted to get right into both of our backseats.

"I can park over there," the grin said.

I laughed out loud. I'd never had this happen before. "Ted? Ted! Wake up. The taxi driver wants to come upstairs with us."

Ted's head rolled around on his shoulders "Okay, bring 'em up," his mouth replied with closed eyelids.

"Are you sure?" I said quietly, closer to his face.

"Bring 'em up!" was the hazy command. I wasn't sure if Ted even knew what he was agreeing to.

The taxi driver somehow parked his car in record time and darted into the elevator with us. He chatted animatedly about his home country of Turkey, how long he had been in Florida, and other random life details he was able to somehow cram into a four-floor ride up. Ted and I leaned against the elevator walls, holding ourselves up. I scanned the driver's burly frame. It was solid in that forty-something, Turkish-wrestler-covered-with-olive-oil kind of way. At least that's what my eyes wanted to see. Where had he parked his cab anyway? When would those damn elevator doors open?

Next thing I knew, Ted and I tumbled into our gross Laura Ashley-inspired suite, landing on the weird floral bedspreads. The Turk cab daddy gingerly closed the door behind him. That damn grin was still planted all over his face. The thing must have been tattooed on. Even though my eyeballs wouldn't really focus for me, I could make out the universal look of a very, very horny man. It was unmistakable, beyond languages even. He probably had a wife and kids at home. Would they stay up waiting for him? Nah, he worked the night shift. He could fuck all night if he wanted to. I wonder if he did? Either way, his face proved that he obviously hadn't been laid in a long, long while. At least he wasn't going to kill us. Just fuck us. Fuck our drunk and half-comatose boy bodies. At least we were now lying down. I saw clothes flying off all around us. I don't know how erections sprung up, but they did. Big ones. Hairy, burly, brown daddy hands groped my boy body. Frantically and thoroughly. It was like they were famished tourists at an all-you-can-eat buffet. Man, were they hungry. I grabbed at his cock and yanked some of his terribly long pubic hairs out of his crotch. He didn't care. Then I went for the cock again, and I got it into my mouth this time. It jammed itself hard into my face. So hard that its 1970s-era black bush or wires scratched all over my nose. It smelled clean enough, at least for a taxi driver, I assumed. I couldn't really figure out the taste of all the precum, with my vodka breath and all the mouth pumping going on. If I had been sober, I'd probably think I was being raped. Orally, in the mouth. But I didn't have the energy or the focus to even care. I just kept my mouth open real wide.

"Yeah, yeah, yeah," an accent above me kept saying over and over again as the thing kept thrusting into my face. Just keep your mouth open wide, it'll be okay. The last thing I wanted to do right now was to gag on the thing. That could start a vomiting chain reaction, and God knew how that would all end. *Not well*, I thought. I felt my jaw begin to ache. Then two hands pushed me down on to the bed, and my pants now somehow came off. Where was Ted, anyway? I could make out a human figure on the bed in the dark. That must be him. Who else? But I knew it wasn't his spit-covered cock that was entering my butthole—this thing felt a lot thicker and hairier and daddy-shaped compared to Ted's awfully cute but rather diminutive little-boy penis. Thank God I was still quite drunk, since my orifice couldn't have been more relaxed and able to take all the insistent thrusting happening all inside it.

"Yeah, fuck me, daddy!" I heard a voice say. It was mine. It sounded kind of sexy.

"Yeah baby, yeah baby." That second voice had a Turkish accent, so that one wasn't mine. Was that Ted's body snoring on the bed-spread next to me? Oh, great. It takes a semi-raping to find out when your friends really have your back. "Ted! Ted!" I said in a super loud whisper. Why was I whispering? Could Mary Poppins hear us from down the hall?

"Yeah?" Ted's body grumbled. I saw it didn't have pants on it. There was a brown man over him now, and I noticed my asshole didn't have a cock inside it anymore. Thank goodness for that.

That thin layer of cab driver spit really didn't work so well. Ted was now lying on his back on that stupid fucking bedspread, moaning like I just was. The poor thing—there was probably even less spit now left for him. Oh well—his body seemed to be liking the thrusts regardless. And that Turkish face was *definitely* liking it, with a grin even bigger and wider than ever. I had to hand it to the Turk dude. He had masterfully bagged two white hottie boys, and in their own room no less. And he got paid cab fare on top of it! And I'm pretty sure I gave him a tip. The filthy lucky bastard. Well, I guess it didn't take a sexual Einstein to figure out we were easy prey, the two drunk sitting ducks laying in the back of his cab. Or drunk gay chicken boys. Or something like that. My head hurt.

The concrete grin was now above me again, and I felt a splash of hot wetness go all over my torso. Then I heard a giggle. Ted was watching daddy semen fly all over me, and this cracked him up to no end.

"Shut up!" I hollered at him, but that just made him laugh harder. I used both my hands to try to brush off the river of daddy cum forming on me, but it just stuck to the hair on my chest and made a big sticky mess. Ted was laughing so hard now I thought he would start throwing up all over the place.

Then we looked up, and the cab driver was standing with all his clothes on and his shoes all tied. Had he even taken anything off in the first place? Ted and I were both buck naked, sitting like idiot ducks on the bed. How were we naked and he wasn't? How did any of this happen, anyway? I felt a trickle of warm semen ooze across my belly and down my sides and on to the thick fire-retardant bedspread beneath me.

The Turkish cabbie person was now all the way to the door. Every time we turned to look at him, it was like he had already moved on to the next frame of the movie. Ted and I just sat there naked, expecting him to bolt in some sort of big grand post-ejaculation guilt-about-my-wife rush out the stupid door. But instead, he smiled that crazy grin and then paused dramatically with the door open.

"See you later, bitches!" was all he said.

The words dangled in the air as the door shut. Huh? Was he trying to be witty and gay, as best a straightish taxi driver in Orlando could be at midnight? Or did he really just fuck us both with just spit, and then call us bitches on his way out the door? With a grin on his face?

Ted and I looked at each other kind of sheepishly in the silence of the room. We then laughed nervously and crawled into bed next to each other. We cuddled together naked, the driver's sperm still sticky between our torsos. We kissed and hugged and touched each other's bodies for the first time in a long time. I felt warm all over, and it wasn't the booze. Or all the semen. It was a long beautiful while before we both finally drifted off into unconscious.

The next day we awoke and glanced at each other, like bitches indeed. Our heads ached, as well as various orifices. What happened? Had we been violated? Was it at least hot? Ted and I had never been so outright slutty in front of each other before, getting randomly fucked by uglyish strangers. Hell, we hadn't even seen each other naked since we stopped having sex over a year ago. Over a heavy hangover breakfast, we made jokes about it all and blamed it on that crazy vodka. The way buds always dismiss weird things that happen between them. That is, buds who pick up middle-aged taxi drivers in Orlando at midnight and take them back to a Disney hotel and then have said driver fuck them with no lube on top of ugly floral bedspreads with Mickey Mouse wallpaper all around. You know—those kind of buds!

The one thing I didn't tell Ted was that for me, it had all been totally worth it. Not the wire pubes or the cab fare or the dangling farewells, but the pleasure of kissing Ted on the lips again and sleeping all night in a nude pile with him and waking up next to him with matching his and his hangovers. For a few nocturnal hours, we were mythical lovers in an unending fairy tale galloping through the dark night. Thanks to an unexpected ride in an enchanted taxicab from Turkey that helped me find such unexpected joy right in The Happiest Place on Earth.

The Ever-Changing Waters of Egypt and the Pacific

We were all standing in Speedos around a pool aboard a cruise ship, while the Pacific whooshed behind us. No land could be seen for miles. We were a portable island of gays traversing the daunting Pacific, clad in barely anything but a thin strip of material over our loins. I was more exposed and vulnerable than I realized.

I was sharing a stateroom with my gay cousin, who introduced me to his poolside buddy. "This is my good friend Mike." Mike was about forty, short, muscular, with brown skin and a goatee and smiling eyes that drank in my tan, lanky body. "Nice to meet you."

"You're hot," I countered, my eyes surveying his bare flesh.

"You too," he grinned widely.

"Let's go down to your room," I proposed.

"Okay!" he agreed.

My cousin glanced over his sunglasses. "For God's sake, I've never seen two guys hook up so fast!"

Mike's premium class stateroom floated above the wide ocean like a cloud. The blazing sun pushed its way through white curtains, and as I moved on top of him the whole room was lit up like a bleached, overexposed photograph. We were amid some sort of imaginary thought, enmeshing ourselves in one another, trying to press into each other in an attempt to become one. I flipped him over, entered his perfectly smooth and round brown ass, and promptly shot my load all over it. I used the sperm as massage ointment and rubbed his butt with my hands, tracing the curves of his tan lines where dark brown skin met beige. My fingers glided over his naked flesh.

But once we came, reality crashed in around our heads, as it always does, and we reentered our own separate bodies. I got up to exit our briefly shared dream.

"No, stay!" He was so instantaneously adamant about it, I automatically crawled right back into bed and pressed myself against his calm, sweaty body. His sweet carnal smell was intoxicating. His ass was stuck to the sheets with my drying semen.

We stayed like this for two days inside his cabin, naked, with streams of white sunlight filling the room. We ordered in food, we napped, we kissed, we chatted. At one point, I even wrote him a moving poem on the back of a piece of paper while he quietly snored on my shoulder.

Mike attached his body to mine for the duration of the cruise, and it felt like a natural extension of my own. Few times in life had I felt this and, even though I am slow to warm up to any new instant romance (which I have too many times seen quickly fizzle and die an abrupt death within the course of a juvenile week), my body was beginning to attach itself to him too.

After the cruise, Mike and I returned to our respective lives in New York, and I curled up next to him in his two-story apartment in Greenwich Village. He worked for a bank, he had money, he was smart with money and math, but all I cared about was being next to his body. We watched movies intertwined with each other, and somehow kept the nascent fire burning. It wasn't as remote or timeless as in his ship's cabin, but I felt incredibly sheltered.

But I was too slow to meet his passion. I felt he wanted to be married to me within a month, and I knew time was the vital and organic ingredient that was needed for us to get to know each other on the molecular level, to move past the wishing plane.

I went to Egypt for a week to write a travel article. Before I left, Mike professed that I was the man he had always been waiting for all these years, that I was the one.

Along with a small group of American tourists, I saw the pyramids, Luxor, The Great Temple at Abu Simbel next to manmade Lake Nasser. We cruised the Nile and almost made it to the border of Sudan. I tried to pay attention to the chatter of the people I was traveling with, but it was blank white noise. All I could think about was Mike.

As I stumbled through the deserts across the great stone monuments to eternity, I saw that time and life were both fleeting and always moving away. My heart finally broke open and I realized I loved him.

Upon returning, I curled up next to Mike once again, the soft, meaty interior of my heart finally splayed open for him to devour. He offhandedly mumbled something about always being there for me no matter what happened.

He drifted off to sleep, but the words rolled around in my head like marbles until I realized he was dumping me, passively yet aggressively.

I woke him up. "When you said that, did you mean we were breaking up?"

He looked at me, groping for words to say.

"Well, does it?" I asked.

He just stared at me. "I realized while you were gone that this wasn't going to work after all ..."

I didn't let him finish. In a daze, I scooped up my clothes, somehow got them on to my body, and staggered into the night, overcome by a storm of tears and a stabbing pain in my gut. The pain lasted for days, for weeks, for months, and I realized that my heart had finally been splayed too wide open too quickly for my own good. I would never be the same again, and I loathed the pain. It was one of those deep, jagged heart wounds that changes the shape of your soul, carving out a part of me that would forever have great empathy for anyone who had had their chest ripped open by another being.

The only image from my Egypt trip that haunted me afterwards was of two of my travel companions, a father and son. They were jolly, fun, and always ready with a joke. One afternoon in Luxor, they rented a felucca sailboat by themselves and set out onto the Nile, all alone. I later learned they had taken the urn of ashes of their late wife and mother out onto the ancient river. They scattered her in the ever-changing waters under the watch of the temples and sand dunes. I scrawled some words on a napkin, thinking of them:

"Go, go, everything must go
Everything must be set free through its own destruction
Everything must always be leaving us, everything must go"

Greenland, the Melting of the Ice Age, and the Coming of the New World Order

I sat in a tiny, sterile lobby of a small hotel in Nuuk, the capital of Greenland. I was watching a man watching TV, and it was fascinating. On the screen, a bare-midriffed Britney Spears hopped into a convertible under a bright yellow sun, green trees sparkling all around her. The man staring at the screen was an overweight Inuit (technically, a Kalaallit) in a black T-shirt and jeans. He methodically took another drag off his cigarette as the smoke trailed up in front of the flat image of the eternal promise of sexualized American youth. Snowflakes languidly drifted just outside the window pane, and slopes of pure whiteness ominously rose up nearby, ready to engulf us at any moment.

What the hell was I doing in Greenland?

I wasn't really sure of the answer. I was beckoned to this, the world's largest island (Australia is a continent, please) during a brief window of time when Air Greenland was inviting journalists to write about their short-lived direct service from the U.S. The idea of Greenland had always loomed large to me, its exaggerated presence on the Mercator world map making it appear bigger than Africa. (Greenland: "Does this map projection make me look fat?") It seemed like a place that no one actually ever gets to, and yet here I was.

You will probably never make it to Greenland, and unless you adore perpetual winter and sheets of ice that stretch on into forever, you won't make the expensive effort to do so. You probably have little to no real idea what Greenland is really like; I didn't either. So I will attempt to paint some sort of personality profile of the place. Worry not—you will be rewarded with a sex scene later, once we get through the necessary exposition. What's a classic porn without a set up, anyway?

It's a complicated thing, this monolithic place with the ridiculous name of Greenland. The first thing you must plant firmly in your mind is that it's really a dream at the top of the world. It's negative space, an empty counterweight to Earth's overpopulated places. It lurks at the summit of the planet, and it's an appropriate launching pad before the top of the globe suddenly leaps off into the cold, dead, unending, unremorseful reaches of space. Greenland is the world before time, the Earth before humans, and the oblivion that reminds you that the realm of reality can easily and quickly teeter off into horrible, horrible nothingness. The emptiness of this landmass feels like it's already halfway there. One feels like a footnote here; your ego is squeezed of its fuel. The towering icebergs, the unending sea, the unimaginably thick ice cap that smothers the island and pushes it down into the planet—it's all on such a severe and unbearable scale that it can crush your soul.

Greenland is the very manifestation of the bleakness of existential angst.

Greenland does not look like it is from our world. It has no trees. It barely has bushes. Nothing grows there except rock and ice. It's a polar black-and-white movie. The island's sparse population paints their houses in crazy Technicolor hues in a futile attempt to liven the place up. Random (and it must be said, overenthusiastic) bursts of neon pink, blue, orange, purple, yellow artificially dot the landscape. But they merely call attention to the fact that they really shouldn't be there in the first place, like a classic movie that has been brutally colorized into a fake acid-trip Easter egg. Humans shouldn't be in Greenland, no one should be there. Wild animals have the real run of the place, basking in some of the last virgin ecosystems on the planet they can truly call their own. Walrus, whales, reindeer, muskox, white foxes, falcons, rabbits all waltz around the island, unobstructed by the pesky human race. One story Greenlanders relished in telling me (especially once they found out I was American) was of a visitor from California who was frying bacon in a trailer. A polar bear smelled the aroma from a mile away. It tracked down the trailer and then tore apart the flimsy walls and opened it up like a Christmas present. Then it went about devouring both the bacon and the woman. To live in an environment like Greenland, a deep sense of dark humor is a mandatory survival skill.

Thus, it was no surprise to learn that Greenland hosts the World Ice Golf Championships every March, held at the world's northern-most golf course at Uummannaq (pop. 1,299) amid slowly moving glaciers and icebergs. Golf balls are painted red so players can find them amid all the ice, and steel clubs are used since graphite ones would snap in half in the cold. How cold? With the wind-chill factor, temperatures can dip down to -58° F. Instead of screaming out "fore!" the golfers probably just quietly freeze to death.

It's strange that humans are even in Greenland at all, since when it comes to a showdown between Greenland and humanity, Greenland invariably wins. The Vikings (you know, those bad-asses best known for their world-class raping and pillaging) hung out in southern Greenland for three or four centuries before packing it up and calling it a day—or dying of famine, as scholars now believe. Their predecessors, the equally tough-as-nails Paleo-Eskimos, also had their butts kicked by Greenland. Around 200 B.C., they too died out for unknown reasons, and for a thousand years, the whole island was gloriously human-free. Even in the twenty-first century, Greenland boasts the lowest population density in the world. Just 57,000 inhabitants huddle around the island's thin strips of coastline in a few isolated towns hugging the western shoreline, pushed to the edges of the icy landmass like mini islets unto themselves. No roads link these towns together. For a landmass of 2.2 million square kilometers, only 64 kilometers of paved road can be found. One lonely airport sees just four international flights a week, all from Copenhagen. They land amid herds of musk oxen and reindeer in Kangerlussuaq, an inland airstrip built during World War II by the Americans, who protected the island during the German occupation of Denmark.

You'll find barely any humans at all in the entire northeastern third of the island, which constitutes the world's largest national park. Covering nearly a million square kilometers, it's hard to get to and rarely visited. Fifty or so hardy (crazy?) souls somehow exist within its boundaries, working (exiled?) at military outposts and weather stations. Even during the height of the incessantly sunny summer, temperatures still can be a bone-shattering -22° F. Winter isn't any more cheery, with over three months of complete and utter darkness. A total blackout, a night that never ends.

As if Greenland in its natural state wasn't frightening enough, the U.S. made sure it would also be radioactive. They carried out one of the world's worst nuclear accidents in Greenland in 1968. A B-52 bomber carrying four 1.1 megaton hydrogen bombs crashed into the sea just off Greenland's northwestern shore, near the U.S. military base at Thule. This happened in January, so thank goodness the ocean was covered with a protective winter ice sheet. Oh, wait. The 225,000 pounds of jet fuel made sure to burn right through that. So that the wreckage and the bombs could end up on the ocean floor. It took nine months, 700 people, 63 million dollars, and a special submarine to clean up the site. Whew, that was a close one. Case closed!

Hang on. Decades later it was revealed that they could only find three of the four bombs. Oops. Most of the details of the whole accident and clean-up were covered up at the time. In the 1990s documents were released that revealed Denmark had knowingly allowed U.S. atomic weapons in Greenland—in direct violation of Denmark's 1957 nuclear-free zone policy. Double oops. Oh, and a lot of the clean-up crew died of cancer, with the survivors suing the U.S. government for compensation. The U.S. of course refused to pay, and still hasn't. Oh, and over half a century later, radioactive plutonium contamination still exists in the area off the northwestern coast. Go America!

Maybe Denmark should just have forked over Greenland when it had the chance. In 1946, the U.S. offered to take the island off her hands for 100 million dollars. But no, Denmark wanted to hold on to her ice cube. And it turned out to be an expensive piece of ice. Nowadays, Danish taxpayers dump over half a billion dollars into Greenland each year to keep the place afloat. And they continue to pay, despite the fact that Denmark granted Greenland autonomous self-rule in 2009. Greenland seems to know how to have its frozen cake with icing and eat it too. It's been trying to get the word out about its new semi-independence, like a proud teenager with their first car. But no one is really paying any attention. The U.N. doesn't recognize Greenland as a nation, and most of the world doesn't even realize people actually live there.

In a perverse way, Greenland reminded me of Hawaii. Hear me out: Both places are isolated outposts of their mainlands, both have a largely mixed-race population of European and Asian (or Inuit) blood, both had been colonized, and both places are known for their natural environment. And both have a deep mystical magic that reverberates throughout their landscape. But only one allows the comfortable wearing of a Speedo year-round, while the other can easily slay you with a flick of its icy finger. And unlike Hawaii's bright yellow streams of light, Greenland's sunshine always appeared to hold dark edges around it.

Let's face it, Greenland is just a mammoth chunk of ice. Literally. At the beginning of my trip, I and the other journalists boarded a bulldozer-like bus once used to carry U.S. Pershing missiles on its back. It looked like it was built to drive on the moon. We were going for an up-close look at Greenland's ice cap. This sheet of frozen water is over 100,000 years old, and smothers about 81% of the Greenland's landmass. It reaches an unfathomable four kilometers deep in parts. The weight of the ice sheet pushes the center of the island down 300 meters below sea level.

Bundled in thick marshmallow layers of ski gear, we stepped out from our weapon carrier on to the slippery surface of the ice and gazed down through its Windex-blue transparency. Down and down it went, like a glass ocean. It felt like cold concrete under my feet, immovable and resolute. But all everyone ever talked about in Greenland was how the whole thing was melting down all around them like a popsicle in a microwave oven. Waterfalls were cascading down valleys that never had them. Unknown islands were popping up through vanishing ice floes. Warmer water fish like cod were being caught where coldwater shrimp used to reside. In summertime, "glacial earthquakes" portended to the inland ice cap cracking and stirring. Greenland is melting at a rate three times faster than it was only a few years ago, and this freshwater runoff has the potential to inundate the Atlantic Gulf Stream, throwing off temperatures for half of the planet. The huge reservoir that is Greenland's ice cap accounts for ten percent of the Earth's fresh water, and once it goes, it floods the world's oceans with a 23-foot rise in sea levels.

This became of mantra of my trip: Greenland is not to be fucked with.

I glided across Disko Bay in a small tour boat, watching the northern hemisphere's most active tidewater glacier giving birth to endless chunks of icebergs the size of buildings. The other passengers and I stood along the deck in our marshmallow clothing, keeping instinctively still as we passed the bergs, as if we might wake them and incur their impassive wrath. We were firsthand witnesses to nature silently and methodically seeking revenge on the puny creatures of the planet. The long-frozen and buried Ancient One from the Great North is alive and it is awakening.

"This bay used to freeze over all the time, but it rarely does anymore," one of the crewmembers told me. His name—Johann Christiansen—conjured a blond, blue-eyed Arian, but his smiling brown face was one hundred percent Eskimo. "In 2002, everything changed."

"What happened?" I hated to ask.

"Everything warmed up. The icebergs got smaller; the fish are different. This place is not the same as it used to be." As he spoke, he didn't look at me, his eyes fixed unblinkingly at the foggy horizon. I couldn't make out where the monotone sky and ocean and snow-covered mountains all began and ended. It was one continuous curtain of unremitting whiteness, and it was terrifying.

So this is where the beginning of the end of the world will happen. Not in a fire ball from the sky, but with a slow drip-drip of melting snow and ice, like Chinese water torture. These fresh water droplets will mix with the saltwaters of the oceans and shut down all currents and the natural cooling and warming of the landmasses and eventually everything will tip over the edge of equilibrium and this is our future. Fuck you, Greenland. Fuck you.

"I remember over fifty people dying in our tiny village from flu in 1935," the elderly Alma Olsen told me. It didn't surprise one bit.

We were talking about the great cosmic menace called Greenland, after all.

I sat in Alma's home as she served me coffee and homebaked muffins as part of the *kaffemik* tradition of feeding wayward travelers. (You never knew when you yourself would be the next traveler asking to be saved.) As she placed the cups on her table, I traced the deep lines of her weathered hands, and they told volumes about what it must be like to be born and raised in Greenland. "The hunters got sick first, and we all almost starved to death because they couldn't get food for us." Her face was stalwart. "That was before we got electricity in 1950."

The tidy, well-heated house had a satellite television buzzing in one corner with CNN droning on about the rest of the world. It felt like a broadcast from another planet. I couldn't figure how the hell humans lived here before electricity. The home's exterior, painted in a blue primary color, seemed aggressively cheery, like a defiant middle finger to the dark and aloof pallor of the landscape.

Alma's thirty-something daughter showed up at the door, kicking the snow off her shoes with a casual indifference. (I noticed Greenlanders treated snow like other people treat air. It's just always there, and they don't really notice it.) She was decked out in classy Danish fashions, and her name—as one would anticipate—was Inga.

"I left Greenland once to live in Copenhagen, but I drifted back here, like most Greenlanders do whenever they go to live somewhere else," Inga tells me in perfect English while sipping her coffee. But whenever she said something to her mother in Greenlandic, and it was both tongue-twisting and soothing. "Greenland is my home. The land here is so thoroughly dominated by nature, it can't help but be supernatural."

I nodded. "Yes, I felt it in the passing icebergs."

I couldn't figure out how this place had such a hold over its people, like some sort of colossal frozen magnet. I guessed they had earned the right to live through the generations; Greenland was allowing them the privilege. Inga could only express her inexplicable love for her brutal homeland in mythological terms.

"We have a sea goddess who lives at the bottom of the ocean and when she's angry—which she usually is—she keeps all the life-giving sea animals to herself down there. We have shamans who have to transport themselves beneath the sea and coax the animals away from her grasp." This goddess' name is Sedna, and she's a bitch. But like most bitches, she has a good reason for being one. Her relatives threw her overboard out of their canoe in order to calm a storm, and her own grandfather cut off the hand that was clutching on to the boat. She sits at the bottom of the Arctic sea, completely pissed. So a shaman has to now totally go out of his way to travel down there and wash and comb her hair for her, which ultimately placates her (the same thing you have to do with most bitches by sending them to the salon). Then she finally gives in and releases the yummy animals for everyone to eat. Inga also told me of the dwarves who live behind the rocks on the seashore, and how the Northern Lights are actually souls hovering above the Earth, waiting to be reborn as children. As a girl, she was carefully ordered to only whisper under their presence, lest the souls hear you and take you up into their heavenly world. Local kids were also warned about wandering off alone among the seashores, lest they be snatched by a Qalupalik—you know, those creatures with green skin and long finger nails—and dragged to the bottom of the sea. It was no surprise to realize the sheer inhumanity of Greenland was not your ideal kid-friendly setting, but when I was told that the ubiquitous packs of pet huskies (found outside of every home) have been known to attack and eat children, I wondered how anyone here ever remained alive long enough to reach puberty.

While trudging through undiscovered regions of Greenland,

Danish explorer Knud Rasmussen asked his Inuit shaman guide about their beliefs. The flat reply was: "We don't believe. We fear."

As night began to fall, Inga invited me to go meet some of her friends at a local bar. We treaded through slushy snow of Nuuk. Streetlights shone around us, and cars slowly threw dirty snow up at us. Inga seemed to know how to avoid it, but my trousers were soon streaked with snow marks. The inhabitants of Nuuk bustled out of a huge modern supermarket, or sat in lit-up little cafés on shiny metal furniture, looking very European. We passed a post office with a huge statue of Santa in front of it, and Inga mentioned that many countries believe Father Christmas lives in Greenland and not the North Pole, and the man receives tons of fan mail here to prove it. The whole town of 15,000 people was well-dressed, prosperous, normal. It wasn't some Eskimo reservation full of sad housing and drunks. It was a sparkling Scandinavian village nestled in the snow. No wonder more than a quarter of all Greenlanders chose to live here. It was Greenland's only bit of civilization, proudly clinging on to the great icy rock.

Inga walked me into a bar called Manhattan. It was shiny and new and there was even a cutout of the NYC skyline on one wall. I assumed this was to indicate that it was a classy place, like New York. Or something like that. It's the de facto gay bar in Greenland, as the "Gayhattan" sprayed-painted graffiti on the outside of the building suggested. There was another nearby bar where gays also popped up. Its name, appropriately, was Daddy's Bar—the perfect place to pick up a gray-haired "polar bear."

We sat up at a glass counter, and Inga hugged some friends nearby. Everyone acted like they were family, and I guess with just 15,000 people in Nuuk the chances were good that they did in fact share some blood lineage, whether they knew it or not.

"I've lived here my whole life, and it's never been a problem for me being gay," Inga's friend Erik Olsen told me as we finished a Tuborg beer. "It's okay here. We're accepted."

Like most Greenlanders, Erik's racial background was part Danish and part Inuit, and his features vaguely resembled both at the same time. He was friendly in a politely distant kind of way. I found most Greenlanders were like that. They probably soaked it from the land itself, which was always right there with you and always just beyond your grasp.

Inga told me that Erik was one of the most famous voices in Greenland. His voice was instantly recognizable to everyone because he read the world news on Greenland's national radio service every evening. Erik's flat yet reassuring voice traveled to the far icy-blue corners of Greenland and reached into fellow countrymen's remote and isolated homes and offices. Through him, they became linked to a grander and more hectic world far beyond their still, frozen shores. But more importantly, Erik told Greenland its weather forecast. In this part of the meteorologically volatile world—where violent storms can whip up in a matter of hours and then suddenly disappear only to whip back up again—hearing the weather forecast can literally be the difference between life or death. Everybody in Greenland felt like they knew Erik. He was their intimate yet unassuming confidant during the long months of silent darkness Greenlanders patiently sat through. And he sat through those days with them.

"When I came out in the national newspaper with a photo of myself, I had people contacting me from all over Greenland, asking how they could get involved with the gay organization I was starting." Erik nodded and smiled, rightly proud of himself. In 2002, he had helped found Greenlanders' Association for Gays, Lesbians and Bisexuals, called Qaamaneq. (As with most Greenlandic words, that's the very overly-complicated way to say "Light.") At its height, Qaamaneq would attract over fifty LGBTers to its house parties in Nuuk. In 2011, over a thousand people showed up for Nuuk's first gay pride parade, followed by a drag show dinner at the country's cultural center. If that can happen in Greenland, then indeed, we are everywhere.

It may sound like Greenland got into the gay acceptance thing late into the game, believe it or not homosexuality was legalized in Denmark (and thus, Greenland) way back in 1933. Denmark became the first country in the world to legalize same-sex unions in 1989, and Greenland was the fourth in the world (and the first in the Western Hemisphere) in 1996. Take that, San Francisco!

I know, I know—you're now wanting to know about the sex scene I promised. What's it like to have sex with an Inuit, do they give Eskimo kisses? Well, I'll never know, because the guy I fucked was a blond, blue-eyed Dutchman.

I grew up in Southern California all around mean, selfish, straw-haired people who implicitly mocked me and dismissed me on the basis of my darker coloring. You can call it hair-based abuse—I do. So instead of fetishizing blonds, I tend to hate them. Their sense of entitlement, their lack of warmth, their arrogant self-centeredness, deriving from the superior God-given color of their head and pubic regions. I never thought of blonds as stupid—on the contrary, I recognized their cleverness, the way they set up their entire universe and the people in it to revolve precisely around them.

So you think I would be smart enough to know not to make an exception for a blond just on the basis of him being from Europe. In my ignorance, I thought his cultured and grounded Eurocentric upbringing would override his blondness. Well, a blond is a blond is a blond, and you can call me racist and a bigot all you want, but the gene deformity that creates that color of hair also creates a superiority complex that can be classified as a psychological disfigurement.

Hans wasn't a journalist, but he traveled with our group to Greenland, since he had a high-up job with a small cruise ship line that ran tours through the Arctic. He was around fifty, and where most blonds age horribly (the one trait that the universe dispensed to ultimately quell their egos), Hans looked pretty good. He was tall, smooth-skinned, and his hair was still a full and light, light blond. He was intelligent, with a good sense of humor. He looked good in a suit. If I hadn't been that taken by him, I would have seen his arrogance from the get-go. But I tend to be blind when it comes to men.

We had gotten drunk one night in a small hotel bar in Nuuk, and before I knew it I was on top of him in his small room, looking at his perfect tan lines bordering a lovely bubble butt as I entered him. He only liked to get fucked face down, lying flat on the bed, and he wouldn't make a sound during the whole thing. I should have known then that it was all about him, and I was just a flesh stick he was using for his own pleasure. In most instances, that's fine with me. But I kind of instantly had a crush on Hans. He was smart, confident, worldly, successful, and smiled a lot. Of course, this is how arrogant people can act in order to have the world revolve around them. And it works. I was soon back a second night fucking him on the same bed in the same position with the same tan lines staring at me. I was even fucking him in a circular motion—revolving right around him.

Hans also lived in New York, and I would call him up when we both returned from Greenland, and after a day or two he would return my phone calls. It wasn't like I was waiting with bated breath for him to call, but the slight distance he put between us just made me want him a little more. Arrogant people do that. He would come to my small apartment (I never saw his for some reason), and he would spread himself out the same way on the bed and I would enter him and get him off and it was all about him. I guess it was my fault too, since I let it be all about him. I felt like a kid in his presence. I guess I kind of looked up to him.

I was surprised when about a month after returning back from Greenland, Hans called and invited me to come to Venice, Italy with him on a business trip. That may sound amazing and glamorous, but I had been to Venice many times since I had family who lived in the region. I was mainly excited to go since I thought it was some sort of sign that Hans really did like me after all. The way he would not pay attention when I told a story, the way he always seemed to want to get off the phone when I called him, the way he always walked ahead of me on the sidewalk, the way he also gave me a smile like you would an infant or a dog—these were just his cultural quirks. After all, he was big and important and I was just so lucky that he gave any time to me at all. Fucking blonds.

Everyone has something to say about Venice. It's one of the few mythical, overwrought places in the world that actually lives up to its allure, its promise, its branding, its hype. The incomparable transgender author Jan Morris (she of the pantheon of twenty-first century travel writers) summed it up nicely: "Venice is a cheek-by-jowl, back-of-the-hand, under-the-counter, higgledy-piggledy, anecdotal city, and she is rich in piquant wrinkled things, like an assortment of bric-a-brac in the house of a wayward connoisseur, or parasites on an oyster-shell." What is left to say about Venice after that?

Morris also wrote that Venice was as "as fruity as plum pudding." I don't know anyone who's ever actually had plum pudding, but Venice (aka "The Queen of the Adriatic") is anything but gay and fruity. There's no queer bar, no gay hotel, and beyond the gondoliers in their lame tourist costumes, the place has no homo whiff about it at all. I read that guys used to cruise in San Marco Square by strolling along the white geometrical lines in the pavement in a special signal to let others know they were available for the taking. But nowadays, it's just all pigeon shit. Venice at its core is achingly hetero. The sorely-missed Ponte delle Tette (Bridge of

Breasts) was where sixteenth-century working girls exposed their ta-tas to boats passing underneath. Advertising pays! The many well-bred and well-to-do Venetian courtesans were artists, poets, and intellectuals. Longtime resident Casanova seduced his chicks in the cafés on San Marco Square, and wrote "Feeling that I was born for the sex opposite of mine, I have always loved it and done all that I could to make myself loved by it."

Venice never struck me as a sexy city. Not even romantic. I guess it's supposed to be, what with its cozily cramped, on-top-of-one-another quintessence and its mystical, mazelike, vaginal structure. But think of any movie or book set in Venice. Only one sturdy thread runs through them all: tragedy, sadness, loss, and a dearth of redemption. Take your pick of movies—*Summertime, Don't Look Now, The Comfort of Strangers, The Talented Mr. Ripley, Casino Royale*. Even the cheesy 007 flick *Moonraker* (one of my personal favorites, naturally) has part set in Venice that somehow feels sad and haunting, despite a slapstick gondola chase with close-ups of pigeons doing double-takes. The best gay novella of all time, *Death in Venice*, is all about an aging closeted gay man who falls into a dark pit of unrequited love with a distant blond boy. Then he collapses in a heap from a plague. (I should have gotten the message about Hans and me in Venice very clearly right there.)

The obvious answer for Venice's melancholic miasma is that it's drowning, sinking, stampeded by untold herds of fat tourists pressing it down even further into the dirty waters. The place is overrun by foreigners who feast upon it like a host of maggots on a long-dead floating and bloated carcass of what was once a gorgeous girl. The sea, the very thing that made Venice rich in the first place, will soon be reclaiming it back as the buildings sink directly into the mud. That's okay—it's poetic justice, and it's a full circle.

The one thing that linked Greenland and Venice to me, beyond the presence of Hans, was that they were both places humans shouldn't inhabit in the first place.

Maybe it's simply the composition of Venice that saddens it. The lapping echoes of water seem to constantly asking for something. The narrow alleyways are darkened, even in summer. Clouds and haze diffuse the rest of the sunlight like an old photograph that has lost its color. Buildings are marred, and from the myriad steps and doorways now half-submerged you are continually reminded of the heights the city once reached. No wonder Mann in *Death in Venice* alluded to a silent gondolier as being a ferryman for the River Styx.

But don't get me wrong. Venice's sorrow is the most exquisite, the most lush, the most cinematic kind there is. It's the melancholy that makes you want to fall back into it, like into a pile of hay or a smelly old duvet. You want to be suffocated in it. You want to linger in the soft, far-away feeling of Venice in a vain attempt to comprehend its opaque meaning. The place is haunted, and in the best possible way.

Fra Mauro, the dude who drew Europe's most accurate map of the world in 1459, never traveled much beyond Venice. Instead, he was given his cartographical information in his dreams via Satan. Then Mauro would project his visions on the low-lying clouds above Venice, like a sort of medieval power point presentation, and copy them on to his map. The clouds were said to take on power of their own, threatening Venice with raging storms and pointing the way to Witches' Sabbath gatherings. Of course, on certain pregnant summer nights the clouds still form over the cemeteries of the Venetian Lagoon ...

Venice is haunted for me too. I first came here with my boy-friend of ten years. I already knew we were on our last legs, but in Venice he treated me like I was his personal tour guide and bank account, and complained about this and that the entire time. I was over it. It was on a boat ride across the Venetian Lagoon where I decided in my own mind to leave him for good. I didn't tell him then, but I began packing the minute we returned home.

I was in control of organizing that trip to Venice, but Hans was the daddy on this visit. Which was fine with me. I tried to be pleasant and cheerful and obedient as a boy should be. But I felt like I was dancing around, trying to make Hans happy, trying to be whatever it was he was expecting me to be. What that really was, I was unsure. So more dancing and guessing. You already know where this is all heading.

Hans became colder and colder, pushing himself deeper and deeper into his emails and his work and the more he retracted, the more I tried to chase him, and the more I lost him. It was a stupid charade I've seen other people fall into as well. One always wants the other more than vice versa. I should know, I've been on the other side of the equation as well. Why do we become devalued to another by liking them, even loving them, so much?

I took to wandering the alleys of Venice, looking in windows, watching tourists, trying not to get lost. And it's nearly impossible *not* to get lost in Venice. I'd eventually make it back to the hotel room, where Hans would be on the phone. I tried to just hang out, I knew this was a business trip for him and I was trying to be an easy-going guest. But I simply didn't know what to do with myself. Hans finally took me to a chamber music recital in an old church and we barely spoke to one another. The music sounded far away and echoed and hollow and I could feel everything slowly moving away from me.

I got sick of calling Hans when we returned home. The last words I spoke to him were: "I am not going to chase you any longer. If you really want to see me, you'll call me. Okay?" They were honest, not bitchy. I made sure of that.

He never called again. I tried to look at the whole thing with Hans as a stock investment gone bad. You try, you loose, you move on. Because Hans was such an abstraction in the first place, I found this a relatively easy thing to do. I never got close enough to finding out who he really was in the first place. Maybe he was nobody.

It was fitting that I met Hans in Greenland, and since then the two entities have merged in my mind into one feeling, one concept, one unbroken space of time. They were both impassable frozen fortresses, neither capable of having a permanent or lasting human mark made on them. Other people are marginalized to the very edges of their existence. I guess that's what makes them so cold and dangerous and alluring.

Epilogue

Something has shifted in the world. Nothing is permanent any longer. Even the structure of the planet is moving, the seasons are off balance, time and space are being condensed and fragmented within the physical world. We humans evolved in a steady, unvarying, timely universe, and that universe of just a few centuries ago no longer exists. Our bodies and our minds are built for a past world, not the one we now live in. And our beings are lagging behind—they have not caught up with this reality.

Humans slip past each other now in an impermanent state of being, like drive-through restaurants. There is less to hold us and bind us, and we see each other as concepts. The individual soul is passé.

But the needs of the heart, the ancient Neanderthal heart that grew up in that cave of long ago, refuse to evolve. They stubbornly cling to bygone modes of survival, and they never, ever give up.